Dancing Through
the Shadows

Dancing Through the Shadows

Theresa Tomlinson

A DK INK BOOK

DK PUBLISHING, INC.
NEW YORK

A DK INK BOOK

2   4   6   8   10   9   7   5   3   1

DK Publishing, Inc.

95 Madison Avenue

New York, NY 10016

Visit us on the World Wide Web at http://www.dk.com

Text copyright © 1997 by Theresa Tomlinson

First published in Great Britain 1997 by Julia MacRae Books.
The text of this book is set in 11 pt. Aldus.

Manufactured in the United States of America.

A catalog record is available from the Library of Congress.

ISBN 0-7894-2459-2

In Memory of My Dear Friend,
Anne Shutt

The author wishes to thank the following for
their kind help, advice, and encouragement:
Christine Chapman, Kath Flint, and Ann Cork,
special breast-care nurses at Sheffield's
Royal Hallamshire Hospital.

Contents

PROLOGUE

It was night. A thick white mist crept through the trees. Ivy leaves trailed from the branches of an elder. Creamy flower heads lightened the gloom, dipping their blooms through the rusting holes in the chicken-wire fence.

Crushed tight inside the small enclosure was a stinking mass of soda cans, potato chip bags, and candy wrappers, steeped in thick, dank mud.

At last a faint light in the eastern sky began to lift the darkness. As the first sharp rays of sunlight cut through the twining elder branches, a gentle sound arose from deep in the ground. Deep, very deep, beneath the filth and rubbish there came the gentle gurgle of running water.

A Fit of the Giggles

All the good things and all the bad things always seem to happen on a Wednesday. The first time I really suspected that something was wrong was also the first Wednesday that we practiced our dancing for the school's annual concert. We were in our second year at Springfield Comprehensive, and Sue Eccles, our P.E. teacher, was in charge.

"Up and stretch, down and stretch. Kick to the side—I said kick, Tracey, not flop!"

We couldn't help it, we collapsed in a fit of giggles at that.

"What's wrong with you all?" Sue demanded. "You're like a load of gyrating elephants!"

Breathless giggles came again. I clutched my side.

"Oh, all right," she said, giving in and grinning. "Ten minutes' rest. Don't worry. It's not really rubbish . . . it's bound to be hard first time."

I sank onto the floorboards, groaning loudly.

"Now then, Ellen, don't fuss." Sue gave me a little pat on the head. "You know you love it really!"

Laura came and sat down beside me. She was flushed and gasping. "Have you brought a drink?"

I nodded. "What's up?" I asked. Laura had her worried look on.

She shook her head and whispered, "I can't do it. Can't get my feet right."

" 'Course you can," I told her. "First time's always hard. Wait till she gets the music on!"

Laura still shook her head. "I think I might drop out before it's too late. Then I won't be letting anyone down."

"Come on," I said. "Get out of here for a minute. Get a bit of cool air."

We snatched up our drinks and packets of chips and went to sit on the grass outside the gym. Though every muscle in my body protested and ached, I *was* loving it. Our concert was going to be wonderful. Sue Eccles taught us wild, fast dance steps, and she made us belt it all out to the latest music.

We got to know Sue Eccles on the very first day that we started school. We'd arrived at Springfield feeling really lost and scared, and we'd been sent into the gym with Miss Eccles. She was the new P.E. teacher, and on that day she seemed pretty nervous herself. She was slim, with wild dark curly hair, and she wore lovely jazzy leotards and bright colored tights. She looked as though she might be a bit of a pushover, but we soon found that was wrong. Very wrong. She laughed a lot and threw her arms around, but she was strict. Her classes were hard work, and there was no messing about in them.

Once the term got going, Sue Eccles started up this dance club, on a Wednesday night, and I've always loved dancing. Well, I couldn't just turn up there by myself, could I? So I persuaded Laura to come with me. It's easy to boss Laura about.

We sat there on the grass at the back of the gym, near the little wood with the smelly mud hole on the bankside. The school caretaker had barricaded it off after the kids had started to throw their cans and rubbish down there.

"We've only got four weeks to practice it," Laura twittered on. "I don't see how I can learn it and be really good by then."

"Four weeks is heaps of time," I told her. "Don't be so pathetic! I can't wait. There'll be our concert and then straight after I'm off to Cornwall. Lovely beaches and sun. Well, there might be sun if we're lucky. Have you ever been to St. Ives?"

Laura shook her head. Suddenly I had a picture in my mind of me showing Laura around St. Ives. We could go poking around those tiny arty shops they've got. We'd walk along the harborside in the evening dressed in our smartest clothes, eating chips and looking at lads. Laura would do anything I wanted. It'd be so much better than just being with my family.

"Hey, do you want to come?" I said. "We've got an apartment that sleeps five, and there's only four of us."

Laura smiled, but she shook her head. "Your mom and dad wouldn't want me hanging around."

"They might," I said. Then I sighed. "They might if I put it to them carefully. My mom's been so cross and grumpy lately. Everything I do is wrong! But . . . I could put it to them this way: You and me could go off around the town together. They wouldn't have me getting on their nerves all the time, being bored and teasing our Johnny. You'd love it there. Blue sea, lovely clean beaches—not like this smelly place," I said, kicking out my leg toward the mud hole. "Oh, there's even a sea lion that comes into the harbor in the evenings. A fisherman feeds him. He's really tame."

"Sounds great," said Laura. Then she wrinkled her nose at the rubbish. "Someone ought to clean this lot up. It stinks, and it's not hygienic. Just turning into a dump. Look," she said. "I've never seen those before. Look at them, little pink flowers, struggling to grow in all this mess."

I frowned, then suddenly saw what she meant. "Oh, yes."

Clumps of pink flowers with dark green spiky leaves were growing all around the mud hole. Delicate flowers with tough green stems.

Laura got up and stuck her hand through a hole in the chicken-wire fence to touch one. "Poor things, growing in among that muck. Ooh, they smell strong," she said, sniffing at her fingers. "Piney."

"Leave them," I said. "I think I can hear the Ecclescake shouting for us. Better get going. I'll ask my mom about St. Ives tonight! I'll ask when she gets back from tap dancing! She's always in a good mood then."

"Yeah!" said Laura.

It was a standing joke between us. Both our mothers had started going to a middle-aged moms' tap-dancing class on Wednesday nights. You should see what they looked like: baggy T-shirts, leggings, fat bums and thighs, with crazy colored tap shoes tucked under their arms. But however ridiculous they looked, it was worth it, for I have to admit that they always came back in a wonderfully jolly and tolerant mood.

"Oh, yes—let them have chips!"

"Oh, yes—they can stay out for another hour!"

"Oh, yes—your friends can help themselves to drinks and snacks!"

We heard the steady thump of loud, exciting music thundering from the tape recorder in the gym. So we scrambled to our feet and ran back to join the others.

2

A Special Dance

The second half of the class was better, just as I'd said it would be. Thudding music filled the gym, and our dance steps started to fall into place. I got that marvelous feeling that sometimes comes to me when I know the routine and the music's good. The blood seems to race through my body, making me tingle right to my very fingertips. I forget any worry that I've got; nothing matters, nothing but the music and the dance.

At last Sue stopped the music and clapped her hands. We all flopped down onto the floor, gasping and groaning.

"Smashing," she said. "I can't believe it's the first practice. Just wish we could persuade some of the boys to join in! Can you think of any who might be willing?"

We all made faces at that.

"You must be joking!"

"What, *them?*"

"Don't think so!"

"Can't see it somehow!"

Laura was pink cheeked and breathing hard, but I was relieved to see that she'd gotten this great contented smile on her face. She wouldn't be dropping out after all!

"Ellen?" said Sue. "Can I have a word before you go? Carol and Janine, would you wait a moment? Now . . . I need one more. Laura, I think. Would you like to be in a special dance, Laura?"

Laura nodded shyly and looked pleased. A whispered ripple of excitement went around the room and a few envious glances came our way. We gathered around the Ecclescake as the others who hadn't been chosen picked up their clothes and shoes and trailed slowly and noisily out of the gym.

"Right," said Sue when our chatter had faded. "What do you know about the Ellwood Vase?"

We groaned. The Ellwood Vase was something we all knew quite a lot about. Skinny little Miss Corrigan went on about the Ellwood Vase at great length in history lessons.

"Come on. What about you, Ellen?"

"The Ellwood Vase is thought to be of Celtic origin. It's ancient and valuable. Nobody really knows how old," I chanted in a flat voice. "It was found when they were digging the foundations for our school."

"Yes, yes! But what has it got on it?"

"Oh. It's got dancers," said Laura. "Dancers in lovely flower-covered dresses."

Suddenly we all smiled and began to understand.

"Yes!" Ecclescake almost squeaked with delight. "You see, I think we need something really different to end the concert. You'll have done all this loud, fast, noisy stuff, and it's really exciting, but I think we need something gentle to finish off. So to make a contrast, I thought we could dress you up like the figures on the vase and make up a lovely slow graceful Ellwood Vase dance. What do you think?"

We were silent then. It wasn't that I thought the idea was dreadful, it was just that I couldn't quite picture what she meant.

"How will we know what steps to do?" I asked.

"First things first." Sue's enthusiasm would not be dampened. "We'll go to the Springfield Museum and take a good look at the vase. What about tomorrow lunchtime? I'll need a note from your parents. I can fit the four of you safely into my Ford, and there's a nice little café in the museum. A sticky bun for everyone who comes!"

We didn't need persuading after that. I thought Sue was probably crackers, but at least it would be something different to do.

That evening I got back home and found the house cold and empty. Mom was usually back from helping my dad in their bookshop by that time. Dad came in half an hour later and started making us a cup of tea.

"Where's Mom?" I asked.

"Oh . . . she had to go into town this afternoon. Shopping. Johnny's gone to Peter's house for tea, so there's no need for her to hurry back."

I frowned. "Oh, I see. Doesn't matter about me?"

Dad grinned and shook his head in the teasing way he has. "*You* are old enough to see for yourself. In fact, I'd say you're old enough to make tea for us!"

"Huh!"

When she eventually came bustling in, Mom slapped a bag of fish and chips down on the table.

"Have to have these tonight!"

"Great," I said. Fish and chips suited me fine, and I wanted to try to get her into a good mood, so that I could ask about Laura going to St. Ives with us.

3

THE ELLWOOD VASE

Later on that evening I waited for Mom to go off to her tap class, but then I realized that the time had passed and she hadn't gone.

I stuck my head around the front-room door. "Half past seven! You'll have to rush like mad."

Mom just shrugged her shoulders and kept on watching TV. "Not going. I don't feel like it. Too tired."

I groaned. If I wanted Laura to come, I was just going to have to ask—good mood or bad. So I tried. I said all the things that I'd planned to say, and I reminded her that Laura wouldn't be difficult or even noisy.

My mother clearly wasn't in a good mood. She didn't say no, exactly, she just heaved a great sigh, as though I'd asked for something totally unreasonable, like a million pounds or the crown jewels.

"Haven't we got enough to do, looking after you and your brother? We've got our hands full as it is!"

"But Mom," I said, "I know we'll have a spare bed. And me and Laura could go off together. I'd be happy! I wouldn't get on your nerves!"

"I can't think straight," she snapped. "I'm not even sure that *we* can go."

"What?" I said. "But why?" This was dreadful news to me, and I couldn't see what she was talking about. "We've already paid for the apartment, haven't we?"

"Yes," she said. "But . . . we're very busy at work. We might have to do other things!"

I didn't know what to say, I was so surprised. My mother has her cross moments, but she isn't usually as grumpy as that. None of it made sense. I got quiet then. Offended.

"I'm not staying here!" I told her. "I'm going over to Laura's to tell her what you've said."

Mom just turned away and went on watching the television. So I went. But from that moment I had a horrid shivery feeling that something was wrong.

When I told Laura how awful Mom had been, she looked worried.

"Janine's mother was grumpy like that," she said. "Janine hated it. Then eventually she found out what was wrong."

"Well," I said, "tell me then! What was it?"

"It was Janine's dad," she said. "He left them and went to live with another woman."

"Oh, crikey!" I said. "My dad did seem a bit funny today. Almost as if he knew that something was up, but didn't want to tell me. Come to think of it, Mom was supposed to be shopping in town, but all she brought back with her was a bundle of fish and chips!"

"Janine and her mother are fine now," Laura told me earnestly. "Once her dad had gone, her mother seemed to cheer up. She went and got herself a job in that new clothes shop that's opened at the top of High Street. She's really enjoying herself now. Her and Janine get lots of lovely clothes really cheap."

"I thought Janine looked smarter," I said.

But that didn't make *me* feel any better about things. I hated the thought of trouble between my parents, and the more I thought about it, the more I knew that something was wrong.

It was good fun getting into Ecclescake's car and driving off at lunchtime. We all seemed to be in a jolly mood.

"Miss Eccles is going to buy us all dinner," I said.

"A sticky bun," she corrected me.

"Sticky buns are not good for dancers," said Janine.

"In that case, you needn't have one, dear!" Sue Eccles told her cheerfully.

The Ellwood Vase had a special alcove to itself, with charts on the walls nearby that showed you where it was found. You could see all the land around our school. The vase was in a fancy glass case; clearly the museum considered it its prize possession. We rushed up to it, and one of the attendants coughed and moved hurriedly forward with an anxious expression on his face.

Sue pushed us aside. "Silence, just for a moment. Let's all have a really good look and see what we make of it."

The attendant moved back, reassured that somebody reasonably capable was in charge.

At first glance, the vase seemed to be just a heavy clay pot; you really had to look quite closely to see the figures. They had funny flat faces as though a child had made them. Each figure faced outward from the vase, with arms and legs in different positions. Their bodies were covered in creamy-colored flowers and green leaves, but parts were worn brown with age. Ecclescake pulled out a pen and pad and began scribbling away furiously, drawing little stick people. Janine suddenly came to life and started talking excitedly about how you could have polyester drapery and green velvet for the leaves.

"That sounds excellent," Sue told her. "You draw the dresses, Janine! Let's have some costume designs."

"There's funny marks around the top," said Laura. "Like Roman numerals, but I can't work them out."

"Runes, I think," Sue told her. "An ancient and mysterious form of writing. Magical, even!"

"Lots of wavy lines around the bottom," I said.

"That's water," Laura told me firmly.

"Could be patterns and zigzags," Janine insisted.

"No," said Laura. "Water."

Miss Eccles looked closely at the vase, screwing up her eyes. "You could be right, Laura. You know, I think we've got just about all the information we need. Come on—who wants a bun? Then we've got to get you back for your math lesson."

We all groaned.

4

WEDNESDAY NIGHT

It was on the next Wednesday night that I found out what was wrong with Mom and Dad.

I came out of dance practice feeling wonderful. The whole thing was going well. We'd tried out our steps for the Ellwood Vase dance, and the Ecclescake put on this weird trickly music. She was full of praise for Laura.

"That's it, Laura. Just what I wanted. Slow and graceful."

I couldn't believe my ears and I pulled a face. Imagine sleepy Laura doing better than me!

We walked home together talking nonstop, and we found spiky little Miss Corrigan, who teaches history and classics, around the back of the gym with the caretaker.

" 'Ello, 'ello," I whispered to Laura. "What's going on here? Do you think they're having an affair?"

"Shurrup!" Laura shoved me, giggling helplessly.

You certainly couldn't think of an odder pair to be having an affair. Miss Corrigan was so small that she sometimes seemed to disappear among the kids. You couldn't ignore her, though, because she's bossy and incredibly energetic. She always looks as though she's dressed for games, in good sneakers and baggy jogging suits, but I've never seen her

actually jogging or doing any other kind of sport. Her clothes
and her size make her look quite young, but her hair's graying
and her face's a bit wrinkled. She can also be very strict in
class. No graffiti on books! Blue ink only! No talking in her
lessons! When she's cross we call her the Corrigan, and when
she's being okay we just call her Corrie.

Our caretaker, Mr. Jones, is younger, but because of his
scruffy overalls and wild hair and beard we call him the
Werewolf.

"What are they doing?" Laura hissed.

The Werewolf was clipping open the wire that surrounded
the muddy dump set into the hillside among the elder trees.
Corrie talked loud and bossy at him as usual, waving a sheet
of paper. Then she began carefully peeling back the rusty
netting as he cut it.

"Oh, come on," I said. "They're both crackers!"

I got home in such a good mood. But again the house was
cold and empty. Not long after, my parents both arrived back
together. I caught a glimpse of Mom as she ran upstairs, and
I was sure she'd been crying.

"What's up?" I asked my dad.

This time he didn't pretend. He looked worried and shook
his head.

"There's something we need to talk about, love, but we're
tired and hungry. Let's get something to eat, then we'll
explain it all to you. Run down to the fish and chip shop for
us, will you?"

"Tell me now!" I said.

"No, it's got to be talked about properly. Explained properly. Will you go down to the chip shop or not? It's just for the three of us; Johnny's over at Peter's house again."

I nodded, and my stomach gave a great lurch. It sounded serious, but I could see that my dad wouldn't budge—and I *was* starving after my dance practice. At least they weren't pretending anymore. That was something.

There was a long line at the chip shop, and Sylvia and Jack, who run it, were having to work fast. Shane Woodhouse and his friends were there as usual. He's in my class at school, and he lives with Sylvia; she's his aunt. He's one of those lads who're hopeless at math and most other things, too. He's always chucking people's bags around, giving lip to the teachers, and making a nuisance of himself. I'd seen Laura watching him with a soppy look on her face. I suppose I have to admit that he's not bad looking; tall and thin with dark short hair. His gang always hangs around outside the chip shop wearing baseball caps turned back to front, hoping that Sylvia will take pity on them and dish out free chips.

"Hiya, sexy," they shouted as I walked past. Then there were whistles and rude remarks.

"Sexy?" I heard Shane's voice above the rest. "She's not sexy. She's just a stuck-up brat!"

"Get out of my way, you idiots," I said, showing them my fist. They melted back. I know them all from school; they're not as brave as they sound.

A warm, comforting smell came floating out of the shop, and I was glad to get inside. Surely my parents couldn't be getting divorced if they sent out for fish and chips before they talked about it? Sylvia was serving at top speed, and she can really move. Cod and haddock flew out from the hot oil, golden and crispy, landing neatly on shelves to drain. The line moved steadily, and there was a tremendous hissing and spitting as Jack poured raw chips into the frier.

The line stopped. "Two minutes for fresh chips," said Sylvia.

My stomach groaned with hunger, despite my worries. I turned away, bored, and watched the lads outside. I wondered what was going on. Shane's head was bobbing up and down in the middle of the gang, with a radio blaring loud.

Then at last the chips were ready, and I reached the counter. "Fish and chips three times, please."

I hugged the hot bundle to my chest as I came out. The gang was still busy watching Shane messing around. I was just about to turn the corner when it dawned on me what it was that he was doing. I stopped for a minute and turned back to watch. He was rolling his shoulders and swiveling his hips, then bobbing right down to the ground and spinning around, his legs whipping in and out so fast you couldn't see them. I've seen that kind of break dancing on TV, and I had to admit that Shane was good. He was very good.

I couldn't stand there watching for long because Gary Hunter called out in a stupid singsong voice: "Hey, Shane. Someone fancies you!"

I stuck my nose in the air and rushed off around the corner, but as I walked up our street a really wicked idea came to me. Ecclescake wanted some boys to dance in our concert. Well . . . if I was crafty, perhaps I could get her one. One who really could dance, though he couldn't do much else. I knew he'd never have thought of it as dancing. It would have to be planned carefully.

I grinned. "You don't know what's coming to you, Shane Woodhouse."

And I didn't know what was coming to me either.

5

A Bit of a Shock

When I got back Mom was putting out plates and cutlery. She looked okay again, but when I was halfway through my fish and chips I noticed that she was hardly eating. My dad wasn't exactly wolfing his meal down either. I took a deep breath and blurted it out.

"You're not getting divorced, are you?"

There was a terrible silence, and then my mother put her hand to her mouth and giggled. I glared at her, annoyed that she could treat my worries so lightly, but quickly the giggles seemed to change to gulping. Suddenly tears were running down her cheeks. My dad leaned across the table, all concerned, and took up her hand.

"It's all right, Jane," he murmured. "All right. No, love—we're not getting divorced."

That seriousness wasn't like him at all; he's usually such a tease.

It was his gentleness to Mom that made me ask her, "Are you ill?"

My mom let go of Dad's hand and wiped her tears away. She drew a deep breath and nodded. "Sort of. I don't feel ill, but I have got something wrong with me. I found a lump in my breast, a few weeks ago now, and I went to the hospital last week to get it checked out."

I caught my breath. I'd seen things about this on TV and I'd read things in women's magazines. I knew it was something that worried people like mad.

"Does it mean . . . ? Have you got . . . ?"

I couldn't seem to say the word, but she said it for me.

"Yes," said Mom. "Cancer. Yes, I have. I've got to go into the hospital and have an operation. And we'll have to cancel going to St. Ives."

"Why didn't you tell me?" I asked.

My dad sighed and rubbed his forehead with both hands. "I'm sorry, love, but we've only really found out ourselves this afternoon. They had to do tests and X rays first. Can't tell you straight away. You have to wait to get the results. We didn't want to worry you if it was going to turn out to be nothing."

"They tell you that most lumps *are* nothing." Mom's voice wobbled. "But mine is cancerous . . . oh, dear. It's a bit of a shock, it really is!"

I didn't know what to say to them. My brain seemed to have gone all numb and blank. I'd known something was wrong, but I'd never thought of this. *This* had never entered my head. Mom said that it was a shock, and I suppose that I was shocked, too; not thinking straight. I got up from the table.

"I'm going to see Laura," I said, and backed off toward the door. Then I turned back to face them again. "Is it a secret?"

"Well . . ." said Dad, hesitating.

"No," Mom cut in firmly, almost angrily. "No, it's not a secret. All sorts of people will *have* to know."

"Will you tell Johnny?"

Mom swallowed hard. "Yes . . . I'll tell Johnny as best I can."

"Ellen, love," said Dad, "don't rush off! We should talk it all through."

I shook my head. My throat felt so tight that it was almost impossible to speak. I couldn't bear their worried faces, so I turned and went.

I walked over to Laura's house, the fish and chips like lead in my stomach.

When I got to her house I stood looking at their mailbox, wondering whether to turn around and go back home, but the door was flung open and Laura's mom, Myra, bounced out, wearing leggings and a T-shirt.

"Hi, Ellen," she cried cheerfully. "Is Jane tapping tonight?"

I shrugged my shoulders.

"Never mind, I expect I'll see her there," she said, and she was off striding down the road at top speed, clutching her tap shoes.

Laura stood in the open doorway looking at me. "What's up?" she asked.

I still couldn't seem to speak.

Laura looked at me closely. "We'll go for a walk," she said, closing the door on the sounds of the TV and her dad asking who was going to wash up.

She took my arm and steered me down the road toward our school grounds. It felt good to have someone quietly take charge; I think I needed that.

"Tell me what's wrong."

"No . . . I can't," I said, because somehow I just couldn't get the words out.

Laura nodded and didn't ask any more questions. She just chatted gently, about Miss Corrigan and the Werewolf. Then as we walked past the gates, Laura suddenly stopped and pointed up the hill toward the little wood that surrounds the dump.

"What?" I asked, almost irritated.

"There's someone up there, dressed in bright yellow."

I stared up the hill and saw that she was right.

"What's going on?" Laura whispered. "Come on. Let's go in and see."

I nodded dumbly and followed her. We crept slowly up toward the wood, and it wasn't long before we could see clearly what was going on.

Laura clapped her hand to her mouth to stifle giggles. There was the Corrigan, quite alone now. Gone was the jogging suit; she was dressed in even baggier yellow overalls and wearing Wellington boots, her hands covered with huge rubber gloves. She seemed to be raking rubbish out of the mud hole. It was so weird.

"What the heck is she doing?" Laura whispered in disbelief.

I felt terrible. I couldn't really be bothered with this crazy teacher. Half of me wanted to rush home to Mom and Dad,

"I told you she was barmy!" I growled.

We moved a little closer, and suddenly Corrie turned in our direction. We froze. Corrie wears glasses, and I wasn't quite sure whether she'd seen us or not.

"Duck down!" said Laura. "Get behind the bushes."

But it was too late. Miss Corrigan had seen us, all right. She put her hand up to shade the sun from her eyes, then said. "Oh, it's you two. Y5 history, Monday at 11."

Laura and I looked at each other, feeling a little foolish.

"Yes, miss," Laura said. "Um . . . we wondered what you were doing, miss?"

"Cleaning up. Can't you see?" she answered us rather sharply.

"But it'll take you ages!" said Laura.

"Yes. I could do with a bit of help!" She sniffed and carried on.

6

A Lot of Them Get Better

"But it's just an old dump," I said. I wasn't in any mood to be patient or polite.

"Now that's where you're wrong," she said. Suddenly she put down her plastic bag and fished in her pocket. She pulled out a bit of paper that was smeared with mud and wagged it about. "Look at this! It's a plan of this area, before the school was built. See the date? 1892."

"What does it show?" Laura asked.

Despite my shocked state I was faintly curious. Vague ideas of buried treasure floated through my mind.

"Look," she said, pointing a dirty rubber-gloved finger. "St. Helen's Well. Even the wood is marked. Ellspring Wood—ancient woodland. I'm sure as dammit that what you call your dump is an important ancient well. Just look at all this wonderful bog rosemary growing all around."

"The pink flowers," said Laura. "I wondered what they were."

I'd never seen Corrie so excited. She thrust the paper back into her pocket and picked up the bag again.

"It's under here," she muttered. "It's under here, and I'm going to find it."

"Well . . . perhaps we could help a bit," said Laura, stooping to pick up a can.

"I could certainly do with it," she replied, almost friendly for a moment. But then she suddenly went all snappy, like she is in class. "Oh, no, no. Not without the proper gear. Put it down!"

Laura dropped the can as though it had burned her.

"Proper gear like me," she said, waving her rubber gloves at us and kicking one of her rubber-booted feet into the air.

"Ah, well," said Laura, backing off. "Another time perhaps."

We hurried off then, back through the school gates, and sat down together on the wall, a bit out of breath.

"Told you she was barmy," I said.

"Yes," Laura agreed. "It's kind of interesting, though. What if there really is some kind of old well up there? And what about her skinny backside in those huge dungarees?"

We giggled together then, and I somehow felt a bit better. Perhaps I could tell Laura now what was really on my mind.

"I've found out," I said. "I know what's wrong with my mom and dad."

Laura waited quietly for me to say more.

"They aren't getting divorced," I said. "I think it might be worse than divorce."

"Worse?" Laura caught her breath.

"Yes. You see my mom's got this lump in her breast . . . and it's cancer. She's got to have an operation."

"Oh, shit!" said Laura, her face all serious.

"That's worse than divorce, isn't it?" I said. "I'm so scared. Scared she's going to . . . die."

Laura frowned for a moment, but then she spoke with confidence. "My mom says there's an awful lot of them that get better nowadays. She should know. There's children where she works that have cancer."

"Oh, yes." I knew that Laura's mom worked as a nurse in the children's hospital. "Children don't get breast cancer, though, do they?"

Laura sighed. "No," she said. "But they do get other kinds of cancer, and I know that they have all sorts of treatments now that can help. They have this thing called chemotherapy."

"Yes," I said. "I've heard of that."

"And Mom is always saying how cheering it is to see so many of them getting better."

"Mmm." I nodded miserably.

We sat there in silence for a few moments, then Laura spoke gently. "Shall I tell my mom?" she asked. "Maybe she could help?"

Tears filled my eyes. "Yes," I said. "Yes. It's not a secret. Mom said it can't be kept secret."

When I got back home my dad was washing up. Mom was sitting on the settee in the front room watching "Coronation Street." Our Johnny was curled up on her knee. They both looked up when I came in.

"Mommy's got a nasty lump," said Johnny, gently patting her chest.

"I know," I said, sitting down beside them.

"She's got to go to the hospital to have it taken out."

"I know."

Johnny suddenly frowned and scrambled off Mom's knee. "Don't want to catch your nasty lumps," he said.

Mom and I both smiled. "You can't catch it," she told him. "It's not like measles or chicken pox."

"Oh, that's all right then," said Johnny, clearly relieved. "I'm going to play football with Peter."

We heard the front door slam behind him.

7

GOING TO NEED A LOT OF HELP

"Now," said Mom, snatching up my hand, "are you all right?"

"I should be saying that to you," I said. My eyes filled up with tears again.

Mom's arms went around me tight, and I hugged her back really hard. We hadn't hugged each other properly like that for ages.

"I don't know what to do," I sniffed.

"Oh, *this* is what you can do," she said. "This is making me feel a whole lot better. Give me lots of great big hugs."

"Are you scared?" I whispered.

She nodded. "Yes, I'm scared. But I think everything's going to be okay ... just hard work getting through it. I'm going to need a lot of help."

"What exactly are they going to do to you?"

"Cut out this cancerous lump and then stitch me up again."

"Just the lump?" I asked. I thought I'd heard of worse than that.

"Ah." Mom nodded. "Yes, it's just the lump. It's called a lumpectomy. Some women have to have a mastectomy done, the whole breast taken away. That must feel dreadful, but if it saves your life I suppose it's worth it. I'm lucky. My lump is fairly small, and it's here at the side. They can get at it quite easily."

"Good," I said. That seemed like something to be glad about.

"They're going to do a test, too," she said. "They make another cut here, near my armpit, and take some lymph glands from there. They can test them to see if the cancer has spread."

I made a face and could feel my mouth getting all wobbly again. I didn't like the sound of that.

Mom took in a deep breath as though she was steeling herself to speak. "Well, it's best to know," she said. "If it has spread, then they can give me more treatment. They're going to do everything they possibly can to get rid of it. They've even given me these tablets that should help. Tamoxifen. I've taken one already."

She took tight hold of my hand again. "Now. What I really want you to do is just try to get on as normal. I don't want this to spoil things . . . your schoolwork, your dancing. It's bad enough that it's messed up our vacation."

I nodded, but I didn't think that it was going to be very easy.

"And there's something else I'd like you to do. Will you come shopping with me? If I've got to go into the hospital, at least I'm going to get some new pajamas. I'm not going to wear my raggy old stuff!"

I gave her a watery smile and nodded. I could do that okay. "When do you have to go into the hospital?"

"Two weeks' time," she said. "The twenty-first. I go in on the Monday and have the operation on the Tuesday."

"But . . . Tuesday. That's the day of our concert."

"Oh, no!"

We both sighed.

"I'm going to be really sorry to miss that," she said.

We sat close together, watching the TV in silence for a while. Then Mom suddenly spoke.

"She's had some kind of cancer," she said, nodding her head at the TV.

"Who?"

"Deirdre. You know, the real actress—Anne Kirkbride. I think it's a few years ago now. And then there's the Green Goddess!"

"You mean the one who jumps around in a green leotard and tights?"

"Yes. She's had breast cancer, and she looks okay, doesn't she?"

"She looks great," I agreed.

We were halfway through our next concert practice before I suddenly remembered Shane Woodhouse and how I'd meant to tell Sue Eccles about him. I hadn't felt much like dancing, but Laura had dragged me there.

"Don't tell anyone at school about Mom," I said to Laura. "I don't want to talk about it, not yet. They'll get to know eventually, I suppose."

"I won't," said Laura. And I knew that she wouldn't.

It was really hard trying to carry on as normal! I couldn't

eat my lunch, and in math my numbers seemed to be jumping about all over the place.

"I can't face dance practice," I told Laura. "I think I'm going to drop out of the concert. My mom's going to miss it anyway."

Laura looked amazed. "You're coming," she said, grabbing me by the arm. "You know you love it. It'll make you feel better."

And she was right. Once old Ecclescake got the music going, I started to feel loads better, and for a little while I almost forgot about Mom and flung myself into it. Then suddenly I remembered Shane.

As soon as the music stopped, I jumped down from the stage to speak to Sue.

"I know a boy who can dance," I said.

"Really, Ellen?"

"Yes. He's great at break dancing. It's Shane Woodhouse."

"Ah." She clearly understood my doubts.

"He'd think our concert was—oh, silly girls' stuff! Soppy, maybe."

"Hmm," Sue Eccles said thoughtfully. "But if he saw what we're doing?"

"Oh, yes! And if he heard the music?"

"You say he's really good? Leave it to me! I'll see what I can do. Try a bit of craftiness!"

I giggled.

"That's better," she said. "I thought you were looking a bit worried and tense. Are you all right?"

I nodded, though tears suddenly sprang into my eyes

again. Even though I liked old Ecclescake, I couldn't manage to explain.

"What was all that about?" Laura asked as we headed out of the gym.

When I told her, Laura went all pink in the face. "You mean Shane Woodhouse might be coming to dance with us?"

"No need to blush," I said.

8

THE MOST PRECIOUS THING

As we walked through the school grounds, we saw Corrie again, brilliant in her yellow overalls and still grubbing around in the rubbish dump.

"Let's just have a look," said Laura, and she dragged me over toward the little wood.

I have to admit that Corrie had certainly made progress. She'd filled four huge black garbage bags with rubbish and was now digging away in thick dark mud with a trowel. She was so intent on it that she didn't seem to notice us creeping up on her.

Laura cleared her throat, then spoke. "Hello, miss! Have you found it yet, miss?"

"What?" She was clearly startled. She got up and adjusted her glasses. "What? Oh, it's you two!"

"Just wondered if you'd found the well, miss."

"Oh, yes! I think I have! I'm sure I have!" I'd never seen her so pink in the face and excited.

"Look at this wet mud," she cried. "I'm sure this is the water source. And see these two stones? I think they're part of the well house. Now look at this!"

She tapped a small flat stone just emerging from the mud where she'd been digging. It didn't look very impressive.

"Now this," she said, striding across to another, similar stone. "And this and this," she cried, tapping more and more emerging flat-topped stones until suddenly we both saw it at once.

"It's round . . . it's a circle."

"Oval, I'd say." The Corrigan looked pleased. She'd made some sort of impression on us at last.

"Feeder pond," she said. "Gathering pond. The water comes up in this corner, under the well house, where it's so wet. Then it should flow into this ancient stone basin. See what I mean?"

It wasn't easy, but we could see that she was on to something.

"It's going to take me ages to get all this damned smelly mud out," she said, quite wild with determination. "I've got to sift it all carefully. Goodness knows what might be hidden away in it. But I'll get there. I'll get there in the end."

"We'll help," Laura said. She didn't even ask me first, and that annoyed me.

"Even if you do find a well," I said, "it's only water."

Corrie stopped work and waved her trowel at me. "Only water? Only water?"

I shrugged my shoulders. I'd clearly said something that she thought stupid.

"What's the most precious thing on earth?" she asked.

We just looked blankly at her.

"Don't you know?"

We shook our heads.

"Not money, not gold or silver, not jewels. It's water. Pure, clean water. Without it we have nothing. Without it there's no life."

She stared fiercely at us both for a moment, then she sighed and seemed to relent. "Oh, well. Never mind. We don't always teach the right things these days. Now if you want to help me you'll have to have boots and rubber gloves."

"We'll get them," said Laura.

"And a trowel each?"

"Yes." There was no stopping Laura.

"I must say, I'd be very grateful. You could be a good help to me."

That's the first time she's been polite, I thought.

"What did you want to say we'll help her for?" I grumbled at Laura as we walked home.

"Well, it's something to do, isn't it?"

"The Corrigan's crazy and bossy as hell," I said.

"I think it's all quite interesting," Laura insisted. "I think it's even a bit spooky, the thought of something really old hidden away down there."

"Oh, great!" I said. "I really want to spend my spare time up to my knees in smelly mud."

"Well, you don't have to," said Laura calmly.

"Oh, no. But you've just gone and told the old bat that I will."

In the end she turned on me angrily. "If you don't want to help, you can just stick it," she said, and she started walking off fast toward her house.

I was amazed. "Wait!" I shouted after her. "Hang on a minute!"

She ignored me and hurried on.

"Oh, *Laura*!" I wailed.

She stopped at last and turned around.

"I suppose I've nothing else to do," I said graciously. "I'll have my tea, then I'll call for you."

9

ELLEN OF THE WAYS

I heard somebody chatting with Mom in our kitchen as I opened the front door. I supposed it would be Myra, but it turned out to be a smart-looking woman I didn't know, sipping a cup of tea. She wore blue flowery-patterned leggings and had blue earrings that swung around.

"This is Kath," said Mom. "She's the special breast-care nurse from the hospital. She visits people like me who've just found out that they've got cancer."

I stared at Kath. She didn't look much like a nurse to me.

"Hi!" she said, very friendly. "You're late getting back from school, aren't you?"

I nodded, and Mom started explaining all about the school concert and how she was going to have to miss it.

"Oh, I'm sorry," said Kath. "That's really rotten for both of you. But we mustn't put this operation off . . . it really is important."

"Yes," I said. "I understand that."

"If there's anything you'd like to ask, please do," said Kath. "It's my job to talk and explain things to our patients and their families. It's a worrying time for kids as well as their moms."

"Mmm." I smiled. "Our Johnny wondered if he could catch it!"

Kath laughed. "That often comes up with little children. Of course they can't. I sometimes think it's worst of all for teenage girls. They worry about their mom, but they start to worry about themselves, too."

I sighed and nodded.

"Try not to worry," said Kath. "It's very unlikely that you would get it, too. Another thing is that by the time you are as old as your mom, we will be better than ever at treating this disease. We might even know how to prevent it by then. And the great thing about your mom is that she's found her lump quickly and come to us for treatment. Now it's full steam ahead to get it sorted out."

"Yes," I agreed.

"Shall I go for fish and chips?" I asked when Kath had gone.

"Certainly not!"

"Thought it would be easier for you," I said. But Mom was fishing around inside the fridge and pulling out bowls of salad.

"I've got it all ready," she said. "Healthy eating! We eat far too much fish and chips. Less fatty food, more fresh veggies and fruit—that's what we need. And whole-grain bread. Don't make that face, Ellen. Go and tell your dad and Johnny tea's ready."

I groaned. I could have murdered for a plate of steaming fish and chips.

"Tea's ready." I put my head around the front room door. "What there is of it!"

Dad grinned. "Don't make a fuss," he said. "It's giving her something to think about. Something to concentrate on instead of worrying about this operation. Sorting out a healthy eating plan. It's making her cheerful and busy."

I could see what he meant, so I didn't grumble. Our Johnny looked pretty disappointed at the selection of food, but he picked up a carrot stick and started munching it.

"I like *this*." He said it with such determination that we all had to laugh.

"Organically grown carrots," Mom told him. "No nasty chemicals in them."

I munched my way through a huge plate of lettuce, watercress, raw carrots, tomatoes, and boiled eggs. It tasted pretty dreary, and it was hard work chewing it.

"It's good food for dancers," Mom insisted. "Packed full of vitamins and minerals, this is. Your Ecclescake would approve."

"Yes, I'm sure she would." I spoke without enthusiasm. "Have you got a garden trowel and rubber gloves?"

When we got back to Ellspring Wood, Corrie was still working away, furiously sifting mud.

"Oh, good!" she called when we arrived. "You've come. I didn't really think you would!"

I still thought she was crackers, but she was certainly more friendly than I'd ever known her to be in class. We waded in, and our boots were soon ankle deep in the smelly stuff.

"Can't we just scoop it out by the bucketful?" I said.

Corrie shook her head and fished in one of her huge overall pockets. "No, we can't," she said. "We might miss all sorts of precious bits and pieces."

She waved a tiny bit of bent, rusty iron at us. I didn't think that looked like anything precious at all.

"Proof—real proof!" She said it as though she'd found the crown jewels. "A bent iron pin. An offering to the water spirits."

Laura frowned and examined the pin carefully. "Do you mean it's old?" she asked.

"It certainly is. Handmade and iron. Could be Elizabethan. Could be even older. They used to bend a pin, so that it wasn't of any further use to humans, then they'd throw it into the well as a present for the water spirits. A sort of thank you for the water, and a gift in hope that they'd keep it coming."

"Doesn't seem much of a gift to me," I said.

Corrie smiled. "With a name like Ellen, you should understand better than most!"

"Eh?" I couldn't see what on earth she was talking about.

"St. Helen's Well," she said. "*Ellen's* Well. When the Christians came along, they changed all the ancient pagan names to saints' names. Ones that were similar if possible. Wells dedicated to St. Helen would have once been named for Ellen of the Ways."

"Who was she?" Laura asked.

"An ancient sort of water goddess. The guardian spirit of travelers' wells. Here we are, just off the old trackway out of Springfield. Every weary walker would have stopped here, and mules and packhorses, too. Even the name of the wood confirms it. Ellspring Wood. Ellen Spring Wood."

My mouth dropped open, and Laura laughed at me. "You should see your face," she said. "It's your well. It's Ellen's Well."

10
FAMILIAR RUNES

I have to admit that after I'd heard about Ellen of the Ways, I started to sift through the mud with a bit more enthusiasm. We worked until it began to get dark and we couldn't see what we were doing anymore. We found six more of the old twisted iron pins.

Eventually Laura spoke with hesitant politeness. "Um . . . I think perhaps we should be going home now."

"What? Oh, heavens!" Corrie said. "Is it that time already? Yes, yes! Your parents will be worried. Off you go. I'll be in trouble for keeping you out so late. I just forgot the time!"

"No," said Laura calmly. "It'll be fine if we go now."

"Perhaps . . . perhaps we could come tomorrow," I said.

"That would be wonderful."

I felt she really meant that. We left her grubbing about in the dark.

As the day of the concert came closer, Sue Eccles insisted that we should start having dance practices at lunchtime. I was going over the vase dance steps in the gym with Laura while we waited for Sue to turn up. Suddenly the gym doors banged open and in marched Shane Woodhouse, with Jamie Fox and Gary Hunter. They were all wearing T-shirts and shorts.

"How on earth did she get them here?" I whispered.

Janine bristled, arms folded. "What'd you lot come for?"

"Exercises. Warm-up exercises. Miss Eccles said."

"We're dancing for the concert," Janine insisted.

"Dancing?" Shane pulled a face. "We aren't doing anything like *that*."

"Huh, no!" said Janine. "You couldn't."

Just at that moment the Ecclescake arrived, carrying her tape player. "Right," she shouted. "No time to waste. Warm-up first, please!"

The boys slunk toward the back of the gym and joined in rather halfheartedly. She certainly put us through a tough workout.

"That's great," she told us. "Right, on to the concert now. You lads can go!"

Shane and his mates moved uncertainly toward the door, but before they'd gotten through, the fast thumping music was on, and we were off, swinging and stamping our way through the most energetic routine. I've got to hand it to Ecclescake: She worked out the timing of it to perfection. I couldn't pause to see what effect it was having until the music stopped. When it did, I wanted to laugh. The three boys were still standing by the gym doors, rooted to the spot, open-mouthed.

"Off you go, you three," Sue called. "Come for the warm-up tomorrow. Unless you want to stay and join in."

The boys hurriedly shuffled off, but I grinned at old Ecclescake. They'd be back the next day, I was sure of it. She'd hooked them like fish.

We spent the evening squelching about in muck with Corrie again. There was so much of it that our careful sifting with trowels would clearly take ages. We managed to lower the level of mud a little, and up near the highest, wettest end we uncovered the top of a flat stone the size of a school desk lid. Corrie spluttered something about runes, pointing to zigzaggy marks.

I got a strange creepy feeling that I'd seen that carved pattern somewhere before.

Laura went absolutely wild. "I said it was water! I told Miss Eccles it was water!"

"What are you on about?" Corrie frowned.

"The Ellwood Vase," said Laura. "It's got the same pattern of runes and the zigzag lines underneath them. I thought straight away that they were supposed to be water."

"Oh, my goodness! Oh, heavens!" Corrie went pale and breathless. I thought she was going to faint with delight as she began to understand what it meant. Then suddenly we were gabbling like mad, telling her all about our visit to the museum and the vase dance.

"We've got some lovely creepy music to dance to," said Laura. "Called something like *A Faun's Afternoon*."

"Oh. *L'Après-midi d'un Faune*," said Corrie.

"That's it," we agreed.

"Brilliant music, by Debussy. Fancy Sue Eccles thinking

that one up. It's all so genuine. There would have been sacred dances performed here. And how could I have missed the connection? Of course the Ellwood Vase is linked to the well. It was probably a votive offering, and it shows the sacred dancers."

"Do you mean it could be an offering to Ellen of the Ways?" I asked.

"Oh, yes," she murmured blissfully. "Without a doubt. And do you realize how old this makes the well? Very, very old indeed. This opens up a whole new aspect of research on the Ellwood Vase." Corrie hesitated. "You know, this makes our well very important. The museum will be interested, and the newspapers. But I'd like to keep it secret, just for a while . . . so that we can get it all cleaned up first. What do you think?"

It was quite funny to have bossy Corrie asking a favor of us. She looked quite guilty about it all.

"Oh, yes," we agreed readily. "Let's keep it secret."

"Just till we've got it all cleaned up," said Corrie.

11

A Daughter Who Tells Me What to Do

I dreaded our teatimes since Mom had taken up the healthy eating plan, but that night I had to admit the salads were really rather exciting. There was creamy avocado, mashed up and sprinkled with nutty toasted sunflower seeds. Chopped strawberries and pineapple pieces decorated the watercress and cottage-cheese salad. Mom had mixed up a wonderful tangy dressing with yogurt, chopped herbs, and garlic.

"I like this dinner!" said Johnny, munching cheerfully.

I had to agree with him.

Mom was flicking restlessly through the paper that evening when she suddenly cried out, "Oh, look at this—the Rolling Stones. They're bringing their show to the new stadium."

"Good grief!" said Dad. "They're coming here?"

"Oh, I've always wanted to see them," said Mom. "Ever since I was a teenager. I nearly went once, but my mother stopped me. Said it was too late to be out at night! I was furious!"

Johnny and me giggled. It was so strange to think of Mom as a rebellious teenager.

"Let's all go," I said. "I know they're oldies, but they're still good."

"Let's see," said Dad, taking the paper from her. "How much does it cost? Oh, help! If we all went it would be a hundred pounds."

"Well," I said. "It could be a special treat."

But Mom and Dad both shook their heads.

"I'm going to have to get someone to help in the shop," said Dad. "Just while Mom's getting better. We're going to be short of money."

I sighed, and Johnny said, "What are rolling stones?"

Shane and his gang were back in the gym next lunchtime right after lessons finished.

"Hey!" he said, flicking Laura's arm. "You gonna show us that dance? The fast one."

Laura looked dumbstruck, and her cheeks went redder than ever.

"I'll show you," I chipped in quickly.

"Okay," he said. "Good dance, that. Just wanna know the steps."

So I worked my way through it slowly, and Shane managed to follow me quite well.

"Come on." He glared at Gary and Jamie. "You, too!"

Then Laura seemed to pull herself together, and she joined in with us. The boys struggled like mad with the steps. I had a lot of trouble keeping my face straight, but by the time Sue Eccles and the others turned up, Shane had gotten it down pretty well.

Sue looked impressed. "Well," she said. "I wouldn't have thought you lads could pick that up so fast."

" 'Course we can," said Shane.

"Want to join in? Better with the music."

"Might as well," he said.

We practiced hard that week, both lunchtimes and after school. The boys learned fast, and you could see by the huge grins on their sweating faces that they loved it. Our vase dance felt a little quiet and soppy after all that fast leaping around.

On Saturday I went into town with Mom. We had a good time looking around the shops for new pajamas for her. We ate a huge and delicious salad lunch, followed by jam doughnuts and cream.

"Well . . . you've got to have something wicked now and again," said Mom, giggling a bit. "So long as you eat healthily most of the time."

We bought two pairs of pajamas. One pair was light green and silky; the others were pink with white spots for when she was feeling better. We bought new rose-scented soap and talcum powder and two new washcloths. Mom seemed determined to find some fun in it all.

Later in the afternoon we went for tea and scones in a rather posh café with lacy tablecloths and waitresses in black dresses and gleaming white aprons.

"Have we got everything you need?" I asked.

"I think so." Mom nodded.

"I keep wondering. . . ." I said, feeling awkward. "I keep wondering. What does it feel like?"

"Oh, a bit scary," she said.

"No," I said. "I meant the lump. What does it actually feel like?"

"Oh, I see what you mean. It doesn't feel like anything much. It doesn't really hurt at all. When I first found it I thought it was probably nothing. That's why it's so important to keep checking your breasts. Have a good feel around." She giggled. "Seems a funny thing to do, but it really matters."

I laughed, too. "Buy yourself some of that rose cologne you like," I said.

"Okay, I will." She smiled at me. "It's lovely having a daughter who tells me what to do!"

12

The Concert

I thought Sunday was going to be awful, Mom just waiting around all worried about going into the hospital on Monday morning. But Dad had other plans.

"It's a grand day," he said. "Come on, get into the car, we're going to drive out to Derbyshire for our lunch."

Springfield is a big industrial town that sprawls on the edge of Derbyshire, so it doesn't take long to drive out onto the moors. Soon you're whizzing through dramatic heather-covered hills and valleys full of higgledy-piggledy gray stone cottages.

We had a huge lunch of roast beef and Yorkshire pudding at a comfortable pub, followed by apple pie and cream.

"Does no harm to treat yourself now and again," said Dad.

Mom just winked at me.

In the afternoon we went on to a small hidden-away village called Tissington. We wandered through the village square in the sunshine and stopped to watch some men hammering away at large boards. They were holding them up by the side of an ancient water trough.

"Oh, look," said Mom. "They're starting work on the well dressing."

"What?" I said.

"Well dressing! Haven't you heard about it? Lots of the villages around here do it. Each well has a special date. They build up wonderful pictures with flowers and leaves and stand them around the well."

"Oh, yes," said Dad. "It's a big occasion. They have brass bands playing, and sometimes they have dancing in the streets."

It all began to feel strangely familiar to me.

"This is just an old water trough," I said.

"Ah . . . 'tis now," said Dad. "But look, can you see water trickling in? That comes from a natural spring. It's been trickling into this trough for hundreds of years."

"Can we come back to see the well dressing?" I asked. "And can Laura come, too?"

"Don't see why not," said Dad, smiling at my interest.

Mom went into the hospital while we were at school in the morning. Dad took us to see her in the evening, after we'd had our tea.

I dreaded going into the grim gray building. No one likes St. Helen's much. "That awful cancer hospital," they call it.

"It's not so bad inside," said Dad, and he was right.

Mom was in a small room with four beds. It was painted light green, and the flowery curtains that could be drawn around each bed were quite jolly. Mom was sitting on a chair beside her bed looking rather small and lost, still in her ordinary clothes. She brightened up when she saw us coming.

"Oh, you needn't have come today," she said. "They haven't done anything to me yet."

"We wanted to see where you were," I told her.

"Wanted to see if your bed was hard," said Dad, thumping himself down on it.

Johnny copied him, and Mom was soon giggling and telling them to stop. "You'll get us thrown out of here!" she cried. But the three sleepy old ladies who occupied the other beds just smiled at us.

We gave Mom some magazines, and Johnny pulled a bar of chocolate from his pocket. She was thrilled with that, even though we knew that she had to starve all night. The sign over her bed said NIL BY MOUTH.

"Does that mean nothing to drink, too?" I asked.

"Nothing after ten o'clock," she said, and made a face. "I'm really going to miss my early-morning cup of tea."

We didn't stay long. We all hugged Mom fiercely. She waved us off cheerfully, but just as we went through the door I glanced back and saw her looking small and lost again.

I hated leaving her there.

The house seemed very quiet when we got back, and Johnny was awkward about going to bed. Dad had to read him story after story. I couldn't sleep that night either.

Next morning there was so much to do, what with getting Johnny off to school and then preparing for the concert, I could hardly think straight. We spent the morning having a dress rehearsal. Our vase dance costumes were gorgeous, thanks to Janine's insistence on floaty cream and white material.

The concert itself was in the afternoon. At last we were waiting for the audience to gather, and I was feeling utterly sick.

"Is your dad coming?" Laura asked.

"Yes." I nodded.

"That's good," she said. "I thought he might have to be at the hospital."

"No," I said. "He's letting Johnny have the afternoon off school and bringing him to watch. They've told us that Mom won't be awake until teatime. Dad's going to leave Johnny with me, so that he can pop in to see her after the concert."

Laura nodded silently.

"They'll have done her operation now," I whispered. "Oh, I do hope she's okay."

"I'm sure she will be," said Laura.

Then suddenly the music was starting, and I just had to put Mom out of my head and throw myself into the dancing.

Laura bumped into Shane in the middle of the fast dance, and I stumbled at the beginning of the vase dance, but apart from that the concert went wonderfully well. As we started our slow floaty vase dance, the audience got very quiet, but when we finished, wild applause told us that they'd loved it. Corrie stood at the back of the hall with Ecclescake, clapping like mad and nodding her head.

"You were brilliant," said Dad, hugging me and swinging me right off my feet.

"You looked like a fairy," said Johnny.

Dad and I both laughed at that, then Dad's face suddenly turned pale and tired looking. "Think I should go and find out how Mom is. Can you cope?"

" 'Course I can."

I pulled my jacket on over the top of my vase dance costume and took tight hold of Johnny's hand. "Come on," I said. "We'd better go home."

13

A Place of Healing

Johnny and I walked home through the school grounds.

"There's a little yellow man up there," said Johnny.

I laughed. "That's no little man," I said. "That's Corrie. You can go and see her if you want."

Johnny ran ahead. "Hello, Corrie!" he yelled in a friendly way.

"Oh, crikey!" I muttered under my breath.

I needn't have worried. Corrie seemed perfectly happy about it. "What a jolly greeting," she said. "You must be Ellen's brother. Where's Laura?"

"She's gone home with her parents," I said.

"Couldn't your parents come?"

"My mommy's got a nasty lump," Johnny told her.

"Oh, dear!" said Corrie, and she looked so concerned that I thought I ought to explain.

"My mom's in the hospital," I said. "She's got breast cancer, and she had to have an operation done this morning."

"Oh, no!" Corrie put down her trowel and folded her arms. "How horrid for her and how horrid for you, too! Is she in St. Helen's?"

"Yes," I told her.

"Damn good hospital, that!" she said. "It's the best place for her to be. There's so much that they can do nowadays. Has she had to have a mastectomy?"

"No," I said. "It's a lumpectomy."

"Oh, good. That's so much better."

She clearly knew exactly what the difference was.

"I thought your dance was wonderful," she went on. "Of course you know what sort of a dance it was, I hope."

"Well," I said, quite puzzled, "it was a dance for Ellen of the Ways and for the well."

Corrie nodded vigorously. "It was a healing dance, too. Long ago they believed that water had the power to heal. That's why they valued wells and springs so highly."

"Could that be true?" I asked. "Can water heal?"

Corrie smiled. "Maybe not in the magical way that they thought. But pure, clean water gushing out from the earth is a wonderful, soothing, relaxing thing. I'm sure that if we can get this well all cleaned up properly, it will become a place of healing once again."

The house felt colder and emptier than ever. I put on the gas fire and the television, and Johnny curled up quietly in front of it, sucking his thumb.

"I'll make us sandwiches," I said. "What kind do you want?"

"Don't care," he said, without taking his eyes from the screen.

He wasn't being troublesome at all, but I didn't like his

quietness. I think I'd rather have had to chase him around the house.

We ate cheese-and-tomato sandwiches, snuggled up together on the sofa watching "Neighbors," and as soon as it finished Dad came back. I was surprised that he was home so soon, and even more surprised at the great grin on his face.

"Right," he said. "Grab your jackets! You can come and see her! Have we any fruit?"

"But . . . I thought she'd be too poorly. I thought you said they wouldn't want noisy children there."

"The head nurse thinks it's a good idea for you to come and see her for yourselves."

Mom was sitting in the chair by her bed, looking just the same as when we'd left her the night before, though she'd got the green silky pajamas on. I couldn't believe it. I'd expected a really sick-looking person tucked into bed.

"Has she had the operation?" I whispered to Dad.

"Oh, yes," he said.

As we got closer I saw that she did look a little different. She was comfortably propped up with a pillow behind her back. Her face was pale and her hair a bit ruffled, but she was smiling at us.

Johnny rushed at her and tried to climb up onto her knee, but Dad caught him.

"Whoa there! Mind the tubes!"

I saw then that two thin red tubes trailed down from

beneath Mom's green pajama top to what looked like a small shopping bag on the floor. Johnny stared at it with interest.

"What's in there?" he asked.

"Blood!" Mom told him in a faint voice.

"You mustn't pull them," said Dad. "They're drains. Mom's got two wounds where they've done the operation, and each wound has a tube to drain away the blood and fluids. They'll help them heal properly."

"What's in the shopping bag?"

"A bottle to catch the stuff that's being drained away."

"Wow!" breathed Johnny, making me wince. "A bottle of blood."

"Does it hurt?" I asked.

"It's really not too bad," said Mom. "It feels a bit sore where I'm stitched, and my arm feels peculiar. It's just as though trickles of hot water are running down the back of it. I keep turning my arm and looking, but there's nothing there."

"Weird!" I said.

"But the main thing is, I'm starving! I missed tea because I was sleepy."

We laughed, and Dad fished around in the bag he'd brought. He pulled out two apples, some grapes, and two tangerines.

"Oh, just the thing," said Mom. She snatched up an apple and started munching it noisily. I was glad to see her sitting there—pale, okay, and hungry.

We didn't stay for long, because once she'd finished the

apple Mom started yawning. "It's been great to see you," she said, "but I think I'm ready for another snooze."

One of the nurses came and helped her into bed. It was a job trying not to tangle the awful tubes.

"We're just going," said Dad. "Give her a kiss, but carefully."

One of the sleepy old ladies in the other beds held out a box of chocolates to us as we walked past. "Go on," she croaked. "I can't eat them."

Johnny dived into the box and took out a handful of sweets.

"Lucky," she said. "Lucky to have such a lovely family to look after her."

I saw that the old lady had a tube and a bag just like Mom's. We thanked her and crept away.

When we got back home the telephone started ringing, and it went on ringing till late at night. I felt sorry for Dad. He looked worn out, and he kept saying the same thing over and over again.

"Yes, she's fine, just a little tired. The operation has gone well, and she's quite okay. Thank you so much!"

"I'll answer next time," I told him.

"Do you know what to say?"

"Yes," I said. "I know it by heart."

Johnny went to bed without any fuss that night.

14

WEDNESDAY AGAIN

We went every evening to visit Mom. The second day she was sitting in the chair in her pink spotted pajamas, surrounded by cards and vases of flowers. Everyone we knew had sent some. She was quite chatty and still hungry. One of the tubes had been removed. We gave her strawberries, grapes, and bottles of fresh orange juice.

The third day she was walking around carrying her little bag with the dreadful bottle of blood. Once she forgot it and tried to walk away without it.

"Ouch!" she yelled. "I keep forgetting I'm attached to this damn thing!" Then we all started giggling.

On the fourth day she was sitting on the bed with her sweater and skirt on. All the tubes were gone, and her bag was packed.

"I'm coming home," she said.

We really enjoyed the next few days. Dad closed up the shop and took the rest of the week off. Mom was cheerful and sleepy and very relieved to have gotten her operation over with. Laura had gone off to stay in Whitby for a few days with her parents.

Typical, I thought. She gets the vacation, and we have to cancel ours. Actually Laura's parents had asked if I'd like to go with them, but somehow I felt as though I needed to be at home.

Still, Dad did his best to make it like a vacation, and one afternoon he drove us to Derbyshire. We went back to Tissington to see the flower pictures and marvel at them. Each well was surrounded by a wonderful work of art, delicately formed like a jigsaw. The dressings were made with hundreds and thousands of flower petals and leaves, neatly overlapping like tiny roof tiles.

"It must take ages," said Mom. "And such patience. Look—each petal, so carefully fixed into damp clay."

"Is it an old idea?" I asked.

"Oh, yes. I don't really know a lot about it, but I do know that it's a very ancient craft."

"An offering for the water spirits," I murmured.

Mom stared at me. She must have thought I was going barmy.

"You see, we're digging out an old well," I told her. "That's what the trowel and rubber gloves were for. It's in the school grounds up near the wood. It's Corrie that's doing it, and Laura made me help, too. You can come and see when it's finished."

Mom frowned. "Corrie? I thought you called her a really bossy little so-and-so!"

I shrugged my shoulders and smiled. "I'm getting to like her now."

*　　*　　*

After the weekend I seemed to notice Mom looking rather worried again. She was back to watching "Coronation Street" once more.

"What's wrong?" I asked, sitting down beside her in front of the television. "You're getting better now . . . aren't you?"

"Wednesday, day after tomorrow!" she said, her voice trembling a little. "I've got to go back to the hospital and have my stitches taken out."

"Ooh!" I said. "Will it hurt?"

"It's not really taking out the stitches that's bothering me," she said. "It's wondering what they're going to tell me. You see, when they made this little cut under my arm they took some lymph nodes out. They'll have tested them, and they'll let me know whether the cancer has spread there or not."

"What if it has?" I whispered, that horrible sick feeling creeping back into my stomach.

"Well . . . I'd have to have more treatment. Quite a lot of treatment, really. They can inject chemical drugs into you to kill off any cancer cells, and stop them from growing. It's a treatment that goes on for months. Chemotherapy—that's what they call it."

"I've heard of it," I said. "Would you have to stay in the hospital?"

"No, not usually. I'd just go in for a day to have the injection, then come home again. Then go back again for another dose after a few weeks."

"Oh, heck!" I said. "How long does that go on for?"

"About six months, I think. It makes you feel tired and

sick, and sometimes your hair drops out. I really hope I don't have to bother with it."

"I hope so, too," I said.

We sat together and watched the wonderful healthy-looking Deirdre for a while. Then another thought came into my head.

"But didn't you say you had to have something else done, too?"

Mom heaved a great sigh that seemed to come from very deep inside. "Yes," she said. "Radiation. That would come afterward. I'm afraid it's all going to take a long, long time."

Mom and Dad were at the hospital for hours the next day, and I went down to the chip shop and bought fish and chips for me and Johnny. When they eventually came back, they both looked tired. I made them cups of tea. I couldn't bring myself to ask what the doctors had said, but Mom told me soon enough.

"Well," she said as she sipped her tea. "There's good and bad."

"Has the nasty lump gone?" Johnny asked.

"Yes, it has," Mom told him, stroking his hair. "It's completely gone and my stitches are all out and everything's healing up well. But . . . just one of my lymph nodes had signs of cancer in it."

I frowned. "Does this mean you've got to have that horrid treatment?"

Mom sighed a huge worried sigh. "It's up to me," she said. "The doctors aren't sure whether I need it or not, so they're offering me the chemotherapy. I can have a little think about it and decide whether to do it or not."

Dad looked as tense and worried as Mom; he hadn't touched his tea. "Whatever you decide, love, we'll all try hard to help, won't we?"

"Ye—es," I said, shakily.

"I'll help," said Johnny.

"It's just that it sounds horrible," I said. "I looked it up in one of your books. It said chemotherapy drugs are poisonous. Don't have it, Mom! Tell her not to!" I grabbed Dad's arm.

Dad shook his head. "It might be the best thing, the safest thing. You've got to remember that it's not Mom they're trying to poison, it's any cancer cells that might just be sneaking around in her body."

Mom shuddered and got a bit watery-eyed.

"I feel so silly," she said. "The truth is, it's not really the thought of feeling sick or tired that bothers me. It's not even the thought of my hair falling out. It's the needles! Lots of injections. That's my real dread. It seems such a stupid reason to be worried."

Dad put his arm around her, smiling and shaking his head.

I understood at once. "Oh, no. It's not stupid at all. I hate injections, too!"

15

SOMETHING TO CHEER US UP

I wished that Laura was around that evening. I wandered down our road feeling lonely and stopped by the school gates. There was a flash of bright yellow, moving among the trees of Ellspring Wood.

"Doesn't she ever go home?" I muttered.

I wondered whether to wander up there and see how the work was progressing, but I'd never gone before without Laura, and I wasn't sure that I could deal with Corrie by myself. Then I realized that if I kept on walking down the street I'd soon be bumping into the chip shop gang. That was definitely out, so I turned in through the school gates and headed for the wood.

Corrie looked up as I approached.

"I've found a second gathering pond!" she said, pointing down the hill to where another, smaller circle of stones was emerging. Then she carried on with her mud sifting. "I think it's the animals' drinking pool. See, this top pool is for people and that's for the pack horses! Isn't it wonderful?"

I sat down on one of the rocks and watched in silence for

a minute. The level of mud had sunk by a good few inches, and I could see what she meant.

"I've also realized what this is," she said, swinging her trowel around and tapping the carved stone that matched the Ellwood Vase. "It's the top of the well house. It's fallen down and clogged up the source."

"Oh," I said blankly. I couldn't understand that bit.

Corrie turned round properly and looked at me then. She put down her trowel and settled herself on another rock.

"How's your mom?" she said.

"Well," I said rather shakily, "she's getting better from her operation, but . . ."

And then goodness knows what happened to me, but I started to tell her everything. Worry just seemed to flood out of me in a great bubbling stream of misery. I told her every detail, the canceled vacation, the hospital, the chemotherapy, the radiation—the lot. She listened and nodded and shook her head. My voice got all choked and wobbly. I started to cry.

"How absolutely terrible for you," she said.

We both sat there in silence for a moment, and I couldn't stop sobbing.

Then suddenly she said, "But you know, you should be very proud of yourselves."

I wiped my cheek and looked up, surprised.

"Oh, yes," she said. "It's a horrible thing to happen, but look how well you're all coping with it. Your mom's done a hard thing! She's found this lump and she's gone right away and gotten treatment for it. That's the best way with breast cancer! You've got to grasp the nettle! Take the bull by the horns! Get it sorted out as quickly as you can."

"Ye—es," I said. "I know it could have gotten much worse if she'd left it."

"And *you* should be proud of yourself. Look what's happened to you. You've lost your vacation, you're worried and scared, but you're doing your best to help your mom. You're looking after your little brother, and though you may be having a good moan to me, you're not complaining to your parents. That's all hard, really hard. I think you're behaving in a very grown-up way!"

I nodded miserably and sniffed.

"You know some women have to go through this all alone, women without children or families. Your mother is really lucky to have you."

I sniffed again and tried to smile. I remembered what the old lady in the hospital had said. Corrie pulled a slightly muddy handkerchief from her pocket and handed it to me. I wiped my tears and blew my nose loudly.

"Keep it," she said.

"Sorry," I said. "Sorry for being such a baby."

"It's not babyish at all," she said. "It's only babyish to cry over nothing. You've got something to cry about. It does you good to let rip. I know that. I have a good cry now and then."

I looked at her, amazed.

"And another thing I do know is that though this

chemotherapy treatment is rather unpleasant, it does work and so does the radiation. There are lots of women who have that treatment and never get cancer again."

I smiled at her. What a very kind person she'd turned out to be.

I felt a lot better after that. And I did a bit of mud sifting and admired the second pool that she'd found. It was clear that she was thrilled with it. When I got back to our house that night, I found Laura's mother there with Mom. They'd just gotten back from Whitby. Myra and Mom were talking quietly, and the funny thing was that I was sure Mom had been crying, too.

"Are you all right?" I said, looking at her carefully.

"Yes,"she said, smiling. "I'm fine. Dad's sneaked off somewhere and I've been having a good cry, but I feel better now I've talked to Myra."

"I've been crying, too. But I talked to Miss Corrigan."

Mom laughed. "Oh, dear! What a pair we are! Well . . . I've decided that I definitely will have chemotherapy. I think it's the safest thing to do, though I hate the thought of injections and needles. Myra says she knows of a hypnotherapist who might be able to help."

"Do you mean a hypnotist?" I asked, amazed. "Like the man on television with the googly eyes who makes people do silly things?"

They both laughed. "No," said Myra. "Nothing like that, and this one's a woman."

"What's all this laughing about?" said Dad, coming into the room.

"Where have you been?" Mom asked him. "You just went out without telling me."

"I nipped into town," he said, and fished in his pocket. He brought out four tickets printed with gleaming silver writing.

We all stared at him, puzzled.

"Four tickets for the Rolling Stones."

"Hooray!" I yelled.

Mom shook her head. "But we can't afford it."

"Blow the money!" said Dad. "We need something to cheer us up."

16

Worrying Has Never Helped

The next day Laura and I went back up to help at the well. It was the last day of our holidays. We spent the whole day sifting mud, and we managed to lift up the carved stone and set it on top of the two bigger stones. Once we'd placed it there I could see what Corrie meant about the well house. The three stones formed a protective little shelter, and water came seeping out through the mud beneath it.

"Just as I thought!" Corrie was pink with pleasure. "This is the source. Quick! Pass me the trowel!"

We watched as she dug away, carefully removing years of thick, clogging mud. Then at last water was welling up and trickling into the oval stone basin that we'd been working so hard to clear.

We set to work excitedly trying to remove the last of the mud. We worked until it was growing dark, then all at once we seemed to run out of energy.

"It's just a big muddy puddle," said Laura.

"Yes." Corrie's voice had gone all flat. "It does look like a big muddy puddle!"

"I thought when the water came, it would somehow be magical," I said.

We all stared forlornly at the dark water's scummy swirling surface.

"Time for us all to go home," said Corrie. For once she sounded tired.

School started up again, and Laura and I went nearly every evening to help dig out more mud. We worked and worked away at it, but years of mud had slowly filled the collecting pool. We found more bent pins, but the task seemed endless.

When I got home on the next Wednesday evening I found Mom lying on the settee in our front room, eyes closed, flat out, with this great peaceful smile on her face.

"Are you all right?" I asked, a bit alarmed.

"Oh, yes," she said in a whispery voice. "I've been to see the hypnotherapist. I feel wonderful."

"Like a cup of tea?" I asked.

"Yes, please!" she whispered.

I brought us both cups of tea, and at last my mom pulled herself upright and sat smiling at me in a slightly embarrassed way.

"Well?" I asked. "What did she do?"

Mom laughed. I hadn't heard her laugh like that for quite a while. It was a real belly laugh.

"She made me feel so relaxed that I can't stop yawning."

"But how did she do it? Did she swing a watch in front of your eyes or make you stare at a magical jewel?"

Mom giggled, but at last she calmed down and told me. "No—no, none of those crazy things! She just told me to sit back in a huge comfortable armchair and close my eyes. Then she talked to me in a lovely, gentle, soothing kind of voice.''

"That all?" I said, almost disappointed.

"Well, it doesn't sound like much, but it seemed to work," said Mom. "She told me to relax and kept repeating it. She told me to let go, let go, let go of all my worries . . . for worrying has never helped. It went on for quite a long time, and I felt wonderful. Then eventually she told me to begin to come back to normal, and I did.''

"Good grief!" I said. "I wish I could hear it all."

"That's the marvelous thing," said Mom. "She recorded it all on a tape, so that I can listen to it every day. The more I listen, the better it should make me feel. You can listen, too, if you want to. Can I borrow your tape recorder?''

All that week Mom listened to her tape, first thing in the morning and last thing at night. A DO NOT DISTURB sign appeared on her bedroom door. I put my ear up against it and heard soft strains of music and a gentle slurry voice. She certainly seemed to be more cheerful when she came downstairs afterward, and that awful worried look had gone.

The following week she went back to the hypnotherapist and came back with another tape.

"This one's specially to help me with the chemotherapy," she said.

"How can it do that?"

"It tells me over and over again to breathe deeply and stay relaxed. It reminds me that the injections are to help me get better. I can imagine the drugs as a white healing light, slowly spreading through my body, burning up all the cancer cells and clearing them away. When they put the needle in I shall take a deep breath and imagine myself in a special place, a place that I love."

"What sort of place?"

"I thought of that little beach at St. Ives. You know the one right in the middle, with the pier alongside?"

"Huh!" I said. "That one's always covered with tourists."

"Yes. But you see the wonderful thing about this is that I can imagine it however I want. I saw myself lying there in the middle of the beach, on a beautiful warm day. I imagined the gentle sounds of the sea and the gulls—and nobody else there at all. The whole little beach to myself!"

She sighed happily, and suddenly I could see her there, too.

17

THE CHEMOTHERAPY BLUES

Mom went off the next Wednesday to start the chemotherapy. Dad went with her. I worried like mad all day and couldn't seem to understand a word our math teacher was saying, but in the evening Mom was back and busily making a healthy tea for us.

"Well?" I said. "How were the needles?"

"It was fine," she said. "Absolutely fine. Just a tiny moment of pain when they put the needle in."

"So the hypnotherapy worked?"

"Oh, yes. I just sat back and listened to the sea."

We all ate our tea together and Mom seemed fine, but toward the end of the meal she started to yawn and her eyes went all watery.

"Oh, heavens," she said. "I can hardly hold my head up!"

"We'll sort out down here," said Dad. "I think you should go to bed."

"Yes," said Mom. "I do feel odd. I think I'm turning into a werewolf."

* * *

Mom didn't turn into a werewolf, but by morning she'd certainly turned into an awful grumpy, tired kind of creature.

I did my best to help by taking some breakfast up to her bedroom, but it seemed everything I'd done was wrong. I took coffee and she wanted tea. I took toast and she wanted oatmeal. Oatmeal in the summer! She demanded orange juice and we hadn't got any.

She was worse still after school that evening, wandering around in her bathrobe looking all pale and ruffled. She grumbled at me for shouting and playing my music too loud, and when I tickled our Johnny and made him scream, she went absolutely apeshit!

She bellowed down the stairs in the most horrible voice. "Just bloody well stop it, the pair of you!"

Johnny looked quite scared.

"She's turned really nasty," I said to Dad.

"It's just the chemotherapy," he insisted. "It's making her feel sick and cross. We must try to be patient. They told us at the hospital that the worst bit should only last for a day or two."

"Good grief. One day like this is bad enough."

I went into my bedroom, but all I could hear was loud, dismal music coming from Mom's room next door.

How dare she tell me to keep my music down!

I recognized Bessie Smith's growly voice, belting out a really dreary song. I know Bessie's one of Mom's favorite blues singers, but that song is really the most miserable you could think of.

Mom's often told me the story of Bessie, and how she

died in a road traffic accident when she was still quite young. Somehow all the sadness of what happened was there in that slow, swinging song.

I couldn't bear it. "I'm not staying here," I said. And I went out of the house to look for Laura.

We followed our usual trail up through the school grounds to find Corrie at the well.

She looked up and smiled at us, but didn't stop her work.

"More bent pins," she told us gleefully. "And a silver coin. I think it's medieval!"

"Oh, good," I said, without much enthusiasm.

"How's things with your mom?"

"Terrible!" I said. "I feel as though I've lost my nice kind mom and some really nasty creature has taken her place."

"Ah, yes," Corrie sighed. "It's the chemo. Mood swings, they call it. I'm sure you'll have your old mom back in a day or two."

"Yes," said Laura knowledgeably. "That's what my mom says. It usually only lasts a day or two."

I looked at Corrie then. "You seem to know a lot about it," I said. "Laura's mom knows heaps. But then nursing's her job."

"Oh, I *do* know a lot about it," Corrie agreed. "You see I've made it my business to know." Then suddenly she laughed and shook her head. "You kids," she said. "You kids are so blooming unobservant."

And I think my mouth fell open then, because she threw

back her shoulders and thumped hard on the right side of her chest.

Laura gasped.

I stared for a moment, then the meaning dawned on me. That side of her chest was flat. The left side had a nice rounded breast, but her right side was completely flat, and I knew what it meant.

"You . . . you," I stumbled. "You have had breast cancer, too."

"Yes," she said. She stopped laughing then and started to tell us about it quietly.

"It was fifteen years ago. They had to do a mastectomy. That was the only thing they could do then. I had a bit of radiation. That was quite difficult in those days—I got nasty burned skin. But do you see? I'm a good example of how well treatment can work! It's fifteen years ago and look at me. I'm fit as a flea."

And she was, I knew that. She'd dig and potter all day by the well and be back there first thing the following morning. It came into my mind then that when she'd spoken about women without families she must have meant herself.

"You didn't have children," I said. "Or a husband. No family to look after you. It must have been horrible."

"Yes . . . it was," she said. "It was a really bad time, but I had my sister to help me and I had a lot of very kind friends. I did feel really terrible about it all. Until I remembered the Amazons."

We must have looked blank. We hadn't a clue what she was talking about.

She laughed. "Don't know about them either? You'll know soon enough if you choose classics for one of your options. The Amazons were a mythical race of fierce women warriors. They come into the story of the Trojan War, with their queen Penthesilea. Well, what I remembered about them was that they used to cut off their right breast, so that they could draw a bow and shoot arrows fast and accurately."

"Good grief." I shuddered at the thought. "Is that true?"

"Ooh, terrible," said Laura.

Corrie nodded. "Dreadful, isn't it! Of course it's only a story, a legend, but do you see? The idea of being like an Amazon cheered me. They were fierce women warriors and they *chose* to have no right breast. Just like me. I began to think of myself as an Amazon woman. I wouldn't be fighting Greek warriors, but like them I would be brave and strong! I would fight my way back to health."

I couldn't help smiling because I'd gotten this funny picture in my mind. Little Corrie dressed in flowing robes, striding around our school with a bow and arrow, threatening big tough lads, just like the Amazon queen.

18

A Bit of Ancient Magic

I sat there quietly taking it all in, but Laura wanted to know all the details. "But . . ." she said, hesitating. "I thought that when women had a mastectomy, they had a sort of—artificial breast."

"Oh, that's right," said Corrie. "A prosthesis. They usually do. I believe they're very good now and comfortable, but in my day they were a bit, well—primitive. They gave me this sort of light pad when I left the hospital, and I was supposed to slip it into my bra. I tried to use it for a while, but I couldn't seem to manage it. The damn thing kept dropping out when I was digging the garden. I do believe that the modern versions are really very good, but I just can't be bothered messing around with them. I'm a one-breasted woman, like the Amazon queen, and the world can jolly well put up with me just as I am."

I sighed and smiled. Suddenly everything seemed hopeful. "Can I tell my mom all that?" I asked.

"Of course you can."

"And will you come and see her sometime?"

"Of course I will," she said rather shyly. "If you think it might help."

*   *   *

I tried to tell my mom about Corrie, but she just wouldn't listen to me properly.

"Oh, I can't deal with one of your teachers coming to visit," she said. "Not now! Specially someone I don't know."

So I went off, offended again. Stuff it! I thought. I'm just trying to help! You can sort yourself out!

We worked very hard the next day, Saturday, and the water in the two stone pools grew deep. Though we sifted and dug, it still swirled with brown mud and scum.

"Do you know, I really think we've done all we can." Corrie spoke in a tired voice.

"It just looks like a muddy mess," I said.

"I think we should leave it now," Corrie insisted. "Maybe time will sort it out."

"Would they have done well dressings here, like they do in Derbyshire?" I asked.

"I'm sure they would," Corrie told me. "I think that's what we need now. A bit of ancient magic!"

I laughed, but something like that had been in my mind, too.

Corrie picked a small bunch of the bog rosemary and attached it to an elder branch with an elastic band.

"There," she said. "There's our well dressing. That's our offering to Ellen of the Ways."

"It doesn't look like much," I said.

"No," Corrie agreed. "But that's exactly what the earliest

well dressings would have been. Just a simple posy, or rags tied to the branch of a nearby tree.''

We went home that night feeling worn out and fed up.

That night I did a strange thing, a crazy thing really, but once the idea had come into my head I couldn't seem to get rid of it. I thought of getting Laura to come with me, but the whole thing was so silly that I couldn't bring myself to ask. It had something to do with feeling desperate about Mom and disappointed about the well. It was supposed to be a wonderful place of healing, but all we'd achieved was two big muddy puddles.

Dad went out that night, and Mom went off to bed early. I waited till Johnny had settled down, then quietly I took my vase dance costume from the closet and slipped it over my head. I found my tape with the Debussy music and put it into my tape recorder, then I crept out of the house.

Ellspring Wood was drenched in silver moonlight and filled with tiny scurrying sounds. For a moment I wanted to turn around and run back home. But then I pressed the play button on my tape recorder and the music drowned out the little scary scufflings. Debussy's creepy melody went trickling through the sweeping branches of the yew trees and elders.

I kicked off my shoes and slowly began to dance. Of course I was self-conscious at first, but the music and the soft grass beneath my feet seemed so right that my worries fled. I twisted and turned, swooped and swirled, filled with a strange wild happiness. So wild that as I swung out my arms there was a sharp rip. I'd caught my costume on one of the twining elder branches. I clicked off the tape recorder, my heart beating fast. There, hanging from the elder branch beside Corrie's posy, was one of my floaty drapes. I reached up to take it, but then remembered what Corrie had told us about the earliest well dressings. Just a simple posy hung on the branches of the trees around a well, or maybe a rag.

I stretched up again and fastened the material securely around the branch. That would be my offering to Ellen of the Ways.

It was then that I heard the most awful sounds. I've never felt so scared and embarrassed. There was rustling in the bushes down the bank near the gym and, worst of all, sniggering.

"Who's the fancy dancer?" A boy's singsong voice called out.

I was caught in a beam of light from a flashlight that bobbed up and down, coming closer.

I snatched up my tape recorder and ran for home. Hoots and laughter followed me, but I didn't stop until I was back at my own front door.

On Sunday morning I woke feeling really stupid about what I'd done. Everyone would go nosing around the well on Monday morning making comments on our dirty puddle. I could just imagine what would be said about the ripped clothing hanging from the branches of the trees.

"Better get that back," I muttered. "Must have been mad!"

I dressed and snatched a bowl of cereal, then headed for

the school grounds. I could see my floating drapery hanging between the trees, bobbing about in the breeze with the rosemary. It looked good there, not stupid after all, and then I noticed the water! I ran to the edge of the pool and flopped down on my knees. The water was clear and clean. I put my hands in and splashed my face, laughing out loud.

Then as the water shimmered and stilled, a tiny face looked up at me. A beautiful green-gray face with delicate dark markings and tiny bulging eyes, gold rimmed like jewels.

"Hello . . . hello," I spoke out loud.

19

THE BLESSING OF FROGS

"What's all this noise about?"

Corrie and Laura were climbing the hill.

"A frog," I shrieked. "We've got a frog! And look at the water! Just look at the water!"

They hurried then, huge smiles on their faces.

"Where? Where's this frog?"

"There was a frog. Honest there was!"

Then suddenly two small plops sounded as tiny bodies dived into the water from the ancient stones. This time two small green patterned bodies did a swift breaststroke across the pool, then raised their funny surprised-looking faces from the surface of the water.

"The blessing of frogs." Corrie's voice was faint with excitement. "And wonderful clear water! What more do we want?"

The frogs made a nervous dash to hide behind the gray rocks.

"But what's happened?" said Laura. "Where have they come from?"

Corrie looked up at my torn drapery bobbing on the branch beside her posy. I felt embarrassed then.

"I did a sort of well dressing," I said. I didn't mention the dance.

"It seems you did the trick. You see! They don't call you Ellen for nothing."

"Real magic?" Laura whispered.

"Oh, well," Corrie said. "You could say that the water's settled overnight and the mud has sunk to the bottom, and you could say that frogs can smell water and come to it from miles around. But I'd like to think that Ellen's brought a bit of magic."

We worked all day, digging up some of the bog rosemary and planting it in the mud around the edges of the pool. Each time we did it the water turned browny gray where we'd disturbed it, but within a few minutes it started to settle down again. We dug up fine gravel from the front of the school driveway and washed it in the caretaker's buckets, then sprinkled it on top of the muddy pool floor.

Laura made a daisy chain and hung it up beside my bit of drapery, making me feel better about my well dressing. Corrie pulled satin pink ribbons from her pocket and made little bows on the branches.

"See. We've all had the same idea," she said. "Of course in the old days the water would be used, and that would keep it clean. Some of it will evaporate, but I think the frogs have the right idea. We could make a lovely wildlife pond."

We both agreed.

Then suddenly Corrie said, "Snails. Water snails, that's what we need, and oxygenating weed to help keep the water clear."

"Where can we get that from?"

"The big pond in Springfield Park."

So we took buckets again and set off for the park. We fished out loads of big curly freshwater whelks and great strands of weed from the pond. We even found a few fat tadpoles swimming around in our buckets.

"Yes, they can all go in," said Corrie.

She bought us sandwiches and lemonade at the park café.

"I think I'm going to choose classics for one of my options," I told her. "I want to hear more about the Amazons."

"I think I'll do it, too," said Laura.

Corrie just sighed and smiled.

By the time it began to grow dark we sat peacefully at the edge, admiring our work. The water was muddy again, but we didn't care. We had faith in it now. It would clear.

"I think we've finished," Corrie said. "There's really nothing more to do. Time will make it grow and thrive. We've just got to keep it clear of rubbish. I think the moment has come for us to go public. I'd better tell Mrs. Jones and let them come from the museum to have a look at it."

I knew she was right. We couldn't keep it hidden away for ourselves forever. Corrie went home, and Laura went in for her tea, but before all the world came to look at our well, there was something I really wanted to do.

"Mom, *please*. Just come have a look at it. I know you'll love it, and it won't take us five minutes to get there."

She was up and dressed but lying on the front room settee,

with old Bessie Smith singing "Nobody Knows You When You're Down and Out."

"I just feel so tired," she said.

Suddenly I felt angry. I clicked off the tape player.

"That's not true," I said.

"What?" Mom was angry then. "If I say I'm tired, I'm tired."

"I don't mean that. I mean that stupid song you're listening to. You may feel as though you're down and out, but it's not true that nobody knows you. I know you, I love you, and I want you to come and see our well."

My voice went all wobbly and my eyes filled with tears, but Mom jumped up from the settee and hugged me tight.

"I'm sorry, love. Of course I'll come and see your well."

I grabbed her hand and dragged her off down the road.

"Steady," she panted.

Then I slowed up, remembering that she was supposed to be sick.

The light was just beginning to fade, and a glorious pink sunset threw golden lights onto the surface of the water. As we reached the sheltering trees I heard Mom catch her breath in surprise.

"Oh, it's lovely," she said, putting her arm around my waist. "Lovely and magical! How on earth did you find this?"

"It was Corrie," I said. "She's interested in wells, and she found it on an old map."

Mom dropped down on her knees on the grass beside the pool.

"Frogs!" she said. "And tadpoles. Pond skaters and water-boatmen! Lovely clean water."

"Corrie says that pure clean water is the most precious thing on earth."

"She could be right," said Mom. She leaned back against the yew tree trunk, her arms behind her head. "This is blissful," she said. "Do you know what's the most precious thing on earth for me?"

I shook my head.

"It's you," she said. "You and our Johnny. You're keeping me going. Even when I shout at you, I still love you. I'm sorry I've been such a pain . . . couldn't seem to help it."

We just smiled at each other.

"You know, I really seem to feel okay again this evening. I'm glad you made me come up here. I suddenly feel sure that I'm going to get through it all."

"I hate the thought of them giving you those horrid injections," I said.

"That part really isn't as bad as I'd feared," she said. "You could come with me next time. Then Dad wouldn't have to miss work."

"Ooh. I don't know," I said, my stomach lurching at the very thought of it.

"Now tell me all about your Corrie," she said, changing the subject. "Did you say something about the Amazon queen?"

20

TOUGH AND STRONG

Back at school on Monday, Mrs. Jones made an announcement in assembly. She described Miss Corrigan's discovery and praised the hard work that Laura and I had put in. She warned that there would be dreadful trouble for anyone who dropped litter or made a mess in the vicinity of the well. I was glad of that.

That week was very hectic. Museum staff came to examine our well. Somebody came from the university and made diagrams and copied the ancient runes and markings on the well-house stone. We even had a journalist from the local paper and a photographer who took pictures of loads of schoolkids by the well.

Jamie Fox and Gary Hunter shouted at me, "Get the fancy dancer in!"

Shane was there, but he said nothing. I ignored them and refused to be in the photograph.

"What do they mean, fancy dancer?" asked Laura.

"They're just ignorant brats," I said, though I knew all too well what they meant. "Just look at them all cramming themselves in front of the camera. They had no interest in it when there was hard work to be done."

Laura looked disgusted. "They haven't even got Corrie in the picture. It's horrible. It feels as though our well has been hijacked."

"Yes," I said. "But Corrie did say to be patient. They'll have forgotten it next week. Then it'll be ours again."

One person who I didn't mind coming to look at the well was Sue Eccles. She walked up there with us and Corrie, that first evening after school. We explained to her how the runes on the well-house stone matched the Ellwood Vase, and that our dance was a very ancient sacred thing. She was thrilled to bits and started skipping and prancing around the well herself.

"I can see it all," she said. "There'd be drums and cymbals and pipes."

"Yes, I'm sure that's right," said Corrie, delighted that she understood.

"We should organize a proper well dressing, with music and dancing." Ecclescake was bursting with ideas. "The art department and the school orchestra could all get involved."

After tea the following Wednesday, I heard this zingy Latin-American kind of tune coming from Mom's bedroom. She'd borrowed my tape recorder again, and a woman was singing fast in a clear bell-like voice. I walked in and found Mom in leggings and T-shirt, jiggling her hips and putting on makeup in front of the mirror.

"What's going on?" I asked. "This isn't Bessie Smith."

"No," she said. "It's Olivia Newton-John."

I frowned. Both the name and the voice seemed familiar, but I couldn't quite think why.

"You know," said Mom. "The one in the film *Grease*. The sweet one who fancies John Travolta."

"This doesn't sound like her!"

"No," said Mom. "But it is. Myra bought this tape especially for me. You see, Olivia Newton-John had breast cancer, and she had a great struggle to get well again. But she made this tape and wrote lots of songs about it all. Listen to the words, they're all about wanting to live and refusing to give in."

I listened, and I saw what she meant.

"They're not sweet songs, are they?"

"No. They're tough songs. Tough and strong."

"Why have you got your tap-dancing gear on?"

"Because I'm going tap dancing," she said. And off she went.

Mom came back that night looking tired but sounding cheerful. She hadn't been home long when a small polite knock came on our front door.

Dad opened the door to Corrie, standing on our step looking very smart in one of her sporty suits, and sounding very apologetic.

"I just wondered? I know it might not be convenient."

Mom jumped up and went to meet her.

"Come in, come in," she said. "I've heard so much about you and wanted to meet you."

Dad and I made them coffee and left them to chat in the front room. We soon heard them laughing together.

"That's good," said Dad. "Sounds as though they're getting on."

"Oh, yes," I said. "I knew they would."

"Thank you so much for coming," said Mom when Corrie got up to go home. "I love your ideas about the Amazon women. Though I've been lucky enough not to lose my breast, I've still got to be brave and strong."

Life seemed to fall into a pattern of ups and downs. Every three weeks Mom went for her chemotherapy and felt ill and fed up for a few days.

Her hair started to fall out, and she had it cut short to make things easier. It filled her brush and comb, and the bath and shower were sprinkled with Mom's wiry locks. But though it came out and came out, she seemed to have enough left on top of her head to look okay.

She still insisted on listening to Bessie Smith's miserable songs when she'd had a dose of chemotherapy.

"I need them," Mom said. "Listening to Bessie somehow gets all the bad feelings out of me. Bessie had a terrible life, but she kept going. She kept singing. She makes me feel as though I can keep going, too."

After a few days of misery Mom was back to jigging around and practicing her tap dancing, while Bessie Smith sang "Alexander's Ragtime Band," in a voice warm as sunshine.

21

St. Mick

The chemotherapy went on all through the summer, and it made it difficult for us to have much in the way of vacation, though we had loads of good days out in Derbyshire.

When the day of the Rolling Stones concert came, Mom was just four days on from her most recent dose of chemotherapy.

The morning of the concert she felt sick and upset. "I don't think I can manage it," she said. "You'd better go without me."

Dad looked disappointed. "But it's meant to be a special treat for you. Look, spend the morning resting in bed, then maybe . . ."

Mom sighed and sniffed and went back upstairs.

"If Mom's not going, can Peter come with us?" said Johnny.

"No," I told him sharply. "Mom's going to come. You and Peter don't even know who the Rolling Stones are."

He made a face at me and went outside, slamming the door.

"Oh, dear," said Dad. "Perhaps it was a stupid thing to do, buying those tickets."

He looked really forlorn standing by the sink in his shirt-sleeves. I went and pushed my arm through his. "No. It was a good idea, a great idea," I said.

"Thing is," said Dad, looking more worried than ever, "I've heard that if you want to get a seat you should go a couple of hours early. Most of the crowd will just stand in the middle of the arena."

"Oh, heck!" I said, seeing what he meant. "Mom will definitely need a seat."

"Yes," he said. "But going two hours early might be awful, too. It's a long time to sit around waiting if you're not feeling very well."

We washed up together and tidied the house, and I took Mom some lunch upstairs.

"Any better?" I asked.

"Not really." She shook her head. "Don't think I can eat much."

But later in the afternoon Mom came downstairs. She'd gotten dressed and put on earrings and makeup.

"I still feel rotten," she said. "But I'm going to try to go. I'll be mad with myself if I miss it."

So we set off early and arrived with two hours to spare, though the stadium was half filled already. It looked as though all the best seats had been taken, but then Dad spied a few seats in a row right up at the front at one side of the huge impressive stage.

Mom and Dad settled down on the seats, and I took Johnny off to look at the vendors and buy drinks. When we got back

Mom grabbed a steaming hot dog from me and tucked into it enthusiastically, ketchup smudging her cheek.

"You seem okay now," I said.

"I think I am," she said. "I feel quite hungry."

"You're not getting fed up waiting?" said Dad.

"No. It's lovely just sitting here watching all the people, the wild clothes and the hair. Look at the stage! What on earth is that huge metal cobra going to do? Oh, say, Ellen, do you think you might go and get me another of those hot dogs?"

So the two hours' waiting really did seem to pass quite quickly and pleasantly. Everyone was in a friendly, cheerful mood, and now and again a gang of people would start off a wave. There was a great roar and cheering as it washed around the arena, making people leap up from their seats, shouting and laughing.

Before we knew it, it was time for the concert to start and a sort of hush seemed to settle on the place. Guitars were tuned and lights flashed. Then the thin strutting figure of Mick Jagger appeared on the stage, and the crowd went absolutely mad. We all jumped up from our seats, yelling and cheering.

Everyone around us started jigging and prancing around as the Stones leapt into action and their music thundered out at us. Johnny wriggled out of his place and stood on the steps beside us so that he could see. The giant cobra blew fire from its mouth, and I turned to see if Mom was okay. She'd jumped up from her seat like all the others and was dancing around, clapping and singing along with the Stones.

Well, she did know most of the words! Even Dad was swaying in time to the music. He grinned at me. We'd done right to come. That was clear.

So I thought, well, if you can't beat them, you'd better join them, and I danced along with everyone else.

The Stones played and Mick Jagger sang and danced and strutted for almost two hours nonstop. The whole crowd sang and danced with him, and so did Mom. I hoped she wasn't going to wear herself out. The show finished with shooting rockets and golden fountains of sparks that sprayed up from the stage high into the night sky.

When at last it had all calmed down and we were going home through the dark streets, Mom and Dad walked arm in arm, still humming songs. Johnny dragged at my arm. He'd suddenly gotten very tired.

"Are you really okay?" I asked Mom.

"Great . . . I feel great," she said. "I could walk for miles. I could dance forever!"

"It's the miracle of St. Mick!" said Dad.

22

NOT SO BAD

Mom persuaded me to go with her when she went for her August dose of chemotherapy. I felt a bit scared about it, but Mom kept on telling me that it would be okay. She thought I'd be surprised, and I was.

I'd never been in the outpatient department at St. Helen's before. When we walked in through the big main doors, I thought we'd come to the wrong place. We seemed to have walked into a bazaar. There was a man sitting at a table with all sorts of teddy bears and stuffed toys for sale. Then next to him was another table with plants and books. Beyond them I could see people having cups of coffee and chatting. Mom laughed at the surprised expression on my face.

"They're raising money," she said. "The League of Friends. They're trying to make the hospital as friendly and comfortable as they can. Now then, blood test first. Come on!"

Down in the blood department a very chatty lady stuck a needle in Mom's arm and took a small amount of blood. Mom was so busy talking she hardly seemed to notice the needle going in. The blood had to be sent off to the lab to be tested, and we had to wait a while.

"Right. Now I usually go and have a drink," said Mom.

We went back up to the coffee place and bought drinks and bags of potato chips. Then Mom led the way outside through a large conservatory and into a wonderful little herb garden, full of wooden seats. Another woman sat out there who'd clearly lost all her hair, but she wore an exotic-looking turban and she waved at us.

"See," said Mom. "This isn't too bad, is it?"

I had to agree. We sat there in the sun, sipping our drinks and sniffing the wonderful smells of mint and sage and thyme, until we heard Mom's name being called from inside.

"I'll have to go and see the doctor now," she said. "It only takes a few minutes. You can wait here."

So I sat there in the herb garden, and she was back very quickly.

"What does the doctor do?"

"Just checks that I'm well enough to have the chemo-therapy."

"And are you?"

"Yes."

The chemotherapy room was another surprise. It was like a big living room with lots of comfortable armchairs and a nice thick carpet on the floor. There were two other women there sitting in the chairs, each with a nurse beside her. It was hard to tell which were the nurses and which were the patients, because nobody seemed to wear uniforms; then I realized that the nurses wore checked aprons over their clothes. Gentle music played on a tape.

"Hi," said a young woman with glasses and short curly hair. "I'm Jean. I'm your chemo nurse for today."

Mom went and settled herself in one of the big chairs. Jean pulled up a stool for me so that I could sit beside Mom, then she brought a stool for herself and sat on the other side.

"Right. Antinausea pills first," she said, and gave Mom two small white pills and a glass of water. She gulped them down quickly.

"Now the worst bit." Jean pulled on thin rubber gloves, then put a soft pink pillow underneath Mom's arm and started stroking the back of her hand.

"She's looking for a good vein," said Mom.

My stomach lurched a bit.

"Aha! There's a lovely little vein," said Jean.

I was amazed at how jolly and matter-of-fact about it all she was. She picked up a fine needle from the tray at her side, and I looked away.

I kept my eyes on Mom's face. She took a deep breath and let her eyelids droop. Her face went all sleepy looking. I knew she was making the hypnotherapy work, imagining herself in her special place. When Jean pushed the needle into the back of her hand, she gave a little huff, then smiled again.

"How does that feel?" Jean asked.

"Fine," said Mom.

"Were you on the beach at St. Ives?" I asked.

"No," said Mom. "I was sitting by your lovely well, listening to the sound of trickling water."

Jean brought out five rather large syringes and carefully fixed them each in turn onto the needle clip in the back of Mom's hand. Gradually the liquids in the syringes disappeared into Mom's veins.

"Does it hurt?" I asked.

She shook her head, smiling. "No. Once the needle's in place there's no more pain. But one drug makes you get a funny metallic taste in your mouth, one feels very cold, and another . . . makes your bottom prickle," she giggled.

"Weird," I said.

"Yes," said Jean. "People have been known to leap up out of their seats if they're not ready for it. Now, this is the metallic-tasting one. Here, have a candy to suck."

She gave me one, too. The chemo took about twenty minutes and seemed to be over much quicker than I'd thought. Mom had to make a new appointment. Then we called a taxi and went home.

"There," she said. "Not so bad, was it?"

"No," I agreed.

Then Mom started to yawn.

23

ALL THE MISERY

The next week was pretty dreary. Mom was grumpy and sleepy, and Dad was working hard to keep the shop going, worried that we'd be short of money. Johnny had gone on vacation to Scarborough with Peter's family.

At the end of the week Myra decided that we all needed something to cheer us up, so she organized a barbecue in her back garden. She invited us and some of her neighbors, and Janine and her mom were there, too.

The food was delicious. They cooked sausages and chicken kebabs, with huge spicy salads, and we finished off the meal with yummy chocolate cake and whipped cream. Mom and Dad sat in Laura's backyard happily chatting and drinking wine as it began to get dark. So much for Mom's healthy diet, I thought.

I wandered around to the front of the house with Laura and Janine.

"That's far enough," Janine said. "They can't see us now!"

"Can't see what?" I asked.

Laura and Janine brought out four cans of beer from behind their backs.

"Here," said Janine, handing me one. "Let's get pissed!"

I took the can and opened it. I didn't really like the strong sour taste much, but I soon began to feel giggly, and it wasn't long before we'd finished the lot. We were laughing so loud that we must have made quite a bit of noise, because next thing I knew Shane and Gary and Jamie were leaning on the gate.

"Hey! What's going on? Get us some beer?" they begged.

So Janine and Laura and me crept around to the back of the house where the adults were still chatting and laughing.

"Are you all right?" they asked us.

"Oh, yes," we said. "We're just getting some more lemonade."

It was really quite easy to help ourselves to some more cans without them noticing. Then we returned to the front of the house and shared our drinks with the lads.

It was funny how it happened. One minute I was all happy and giggly and enjoying myself, the next moment I started to feel sad.

"What's up with you?" Gary asked.

There was a silence, then Janine spoke. "She'll be worried about her mom," she said.

"What's up?"

"She's not very well. She's got breast cancer," I told him.

"Oh, shit!" he gasped.

"What you lot on about?" said Shane.

"Ellen's mom's got breast cancer," Janine repeated. "My mom's friend had it, you know . . . she died. They thought she was getting better, but then suddenly one Christmas she just collapsed and died. Don't know what I'd do if my mom died."

I started to shiver. That awful heavy feeling of sadness and panic grew stronger and stronger. I thought it was going to swamp me.

"You stupid idiot!" said Laura to Janine.

"What? Oh, I didn't mean—"

"You would manage if your mom died," said Shane calmly. "My parents are both dead. But I manage. I've got Sylvia."

Gary and Jamie shuffled toward the gate. They clearly thought the fun was turning sour.

"Come on," Gary said to Shane. "I'm off."

Shane hesitated by the gate.

"Are you all right?" he said to me kindly.

His unexpected kindness seemed to upset me even more. I could see Laura's face looking all pale and worried in the moonlight. Suddenly I was crying, and I couldn't stop. Great howling sobs tore from me.

"Oh, heck," said Janine. "I didn't mean. . . . Sorry . . . I'm sorry."

Laura grabbed hold of my arm and rubbed my back.

"S'all right, s'all right," she said.

Then suddenly the side gate opened and Myra came out to us, carrying a camping light.

"What's all this noise? Whatever's wrong?"

I saw my mom hovering behind her, and I just ran and hurled myself at her, howling and crying like mad.

"What is it?" Mom asked. "Whatever is it?"

"Don't die! Don't die!" I cried. "Don't die, please don't die!"

"Ah!" she sighed, and I felt her arms go around me tight. "Hush! Hush!" she said. "Calm down."

Myra's foot caught one of the empty cans, and she stooped to pick it up.

"Look, Jane," she said. "They've been drinking. This is the booze talking!"

"You daft kids!" said Mom.

"Promise me!" I bellowed. "Promise me you won't die."

"Now look!" said Mom, stroking my hair. "Now listen. I can't promise you that. We've all got to die sometime. What I can promise you is this. I'm doing everything I possibly can to get better and stay alive for a long time. That's why I'm having all this treatment. I'm really doing the very best I can. Now hush, love!"

Slowly my sobbing calmed, and Myra came close and wrapped her arms around us both. Laura came pushing into the huddle and we all four stood there hugging each other quietly. Thank goodness the boys had left!

Dad came through from the back. He stopped and stared at us. "What's going on?" he asked. "Are you all right?"

I think it was Mom who laughed first. Then suddenly we were all giggling and wiping tears from our eyes.

"Yes, we're fine," said Mom. "We're absolutely fine. But I really think it's time we went home."

Next morning I woke with a thumping headache. I remembered what had happened and felt guilty and foolish. As soon as I heard Dad go downstairs I crept along the landing to Mom's room. She was sitting up in bed, sipping a cup of tea.

I stood by the door hanging on to the doorknob.

"I'm sorry," I said, all shamefaced and stupid.

Mom pulled aside the quilt and patted the bed.

"Come on," she said. "Come and snuggle in."

So though I hadn't done that for ages, I went and climbed into bed beside her.

"It's all okay," she said, putting her arm around me.

"But I upset you, didn't I? Talking about dying and that?"

"Nothing I haven't been thinking about anyway," she said. "But it would have been better if we'd had a proper talk instead of you getting into such a state. I'm worried about you drinking alcohol."

"The others were doing it," I said, knowing it sounded childish.

"Do you have to do everything they do?"

"No," I said and shook my head. "I thought beer was supposed to make you feel cheerful, but last night it seemed to make me as miserable as can be."

Mom smiled. "Yes. Sometimes it brings out all the misery of the world. Now look here. You are a strong person, Ellen. Promise me you won't drink again just because everyone else is."

"I promise," I said, and hugged her tight.

24

END OF THE HOLIDAY

Laura went off to Whitby again, and though Myra offered to take me with them I chose to stay at home. It seemed as if everyone had gone away. Even Corrie had gone on a youth-hosteling trek into Derbyshire, tramping from village to village, studying the ancient wells. Youth hosteling! I ask you!

Mom and I had some nice days out together. We went shopping in town, and we went to Bakewell market, and then we had a lovely sunny afternoon in Chatsworth gardens. But when Mom had had her chemotherapy I was lonely and bored, wishing then that I'd gone away with Laura.

I wandered down to the shop to help Dad for a while, but I got fed up with that and went up to the well. Sitting there soothed me a bit. The creamy elderflowers had gone, and in their place green and black berries hung. All the tadpoles had turned into tiny frogs; perfect in every detail, but only as big as my thumbnail. They hopped about madly in all directions, delighted to discover what powerful back legs they'd got. Ferns and grass had crept to the edges of the pools, making it all look green and lush. I leaned back in the sunshine, listening to the happy croaking and gentle gurgle of water.

But I didn't have peace for long!

I sat up sharply at the sound of dry wood cracking, and I saw Shane Woodhouse peeping at me through the elder leaves. That was the last thing I needed. Shane and the chip shop gang.

"What are you doing here?" I asked.

He came out from behind the bush. At least there didn't seem to be Jamie or Gary with him. "Nothing," he said. "Bored. What're you doing?"

"Listening to the frogs," I said.

"Frogs?" He looked around almost nervously.

"Yes. They're lovely," I said, and pointed to where two tiny froglets perched on an old mossy stone. Suddenly they both dived into the water with resounding plops.

"Bloody hell!" said Shane. "They're great. I haven't seen them before."

"Where're your mates?" I asked.

"Gone away. Jamie's in Torremolinos, and Gary's gone with him. They're not back till term starts now. Where's dopey Laura?"

I frowned. "Don't call her that!" I said, then I giggled. "Same thing! But she's gone to Whitby."

"Boring, isn't it," he said, and he sat down and dabbled his hand in the water, making the frogs panic and swim frantically to hide.

We just sat there quietly for a moment then he suddenly said. "I saw you! Saw you dancing, in the dark."

Oh, shit! I thought. Now he's going to make me feel like a complete fool.

"It was good," he said.

I looked at him. Was he making fun?

"It was really good," he said. "Creepy—that music. It made me go all shivery. They were scared, too, at first. Thought they'd seen a ghost. Gave me shivers all down my back."

He didn't seem to be joking.

"You're good at that dancing," he said.

"Well, so are you," I said. I took a deep breath. "It was me told Sue Eccles that you could dance." Then suddenly I was telling him all about how we'd conned him into the dance practice on purpose.

"You crafty bitches!" he said. But he looked quite pleased.

"Why don't you come to the dance club when term starts up again? It's right good fun. Ecclescake shouts and yells at us and it's hard work, but it's great."

"I might. Any lads go?"

I shook my head.

"I'll have to get Jamie and Gary to come," he said.

We sat there in silence for a while. Then he said awkwardly, "I'm sorry your mom's been poorly. You were really upset, weren't you?"

"It's all right," I said. "I think she's going to be okay."

I told him about all the treatment she was having.

"Sounds horrible," he said. "Do you want to come down to the chip shop with me? Sylvia'll give us free chips."

"Okay," I said.

*   *   *

So the last part of the summer holidays was very strange and different. I seemed to spend quite a lot of time hanging around outside the chip shop with Shane, then we'd go and sit by the well. He showed me how to do some of his brilliant break dancing, and I really got to like him.

When term started it was awkward. Suddenly he was back with his mates and I was back with Laura. But the first Wednesday night he turned up at the dance club with Jamie and Gary. They all joined in, and Ecclescake kept grinning at me. I could see she was thrilled to pieces to get three lads in the group.

25

EVERYONE'S GOT BORED

The chemotherapy went on through September and October. Mom was really glad when she'd had her last dose, even though she knew she was going to feel sick for a few days.

All through October they had special programs on TV about breast cancer, and people who were concerned about it went around with little pink ribbons pinned to their coats. Laura brought some to our house. Mom snatched one up and fixed it to her jacket.

"Do you want one?" said Laura to me.

"Ooh! I don't know. Everyone'll notice it."

"That's the whole point," said Laura. "There's pink postcards, too. The idea is to get as many people as you can to send a postcard off to the prime minister. It's to let him know that you think the government should spend more money on research and treatment for breast cancer."

"I *do* want that to happen," I said.

"You don't *have* to wear one," said Mom. "Only if you feel okay about it."

I picked one up and fastened it to my sweater. It seemed that even Laura was braver than me.

*   *   *

We went off to school together wearing our pink ribbons, and the first lesson we had was classics with Corrie. There she was, standing at the front of the class with a large pink ribbon pinned onto her flat chest.

I thought, if she can do that, then I can certainly wear my pink ribbon, too.

People did look at us curiously, but once we'd explained what it was all about other kids began to say nice things.

"Good for you!"

"Well done!"

"Ooh, I want one of them!"

"Can I send a pink postcard?"

Gradually pink ribbons began to spring up all around school. Both kids and teachers started to wear them. One Wednesday when Shane came to dance club I saw that he was wearing one. The next day so were Gary and Jamie.

At the end of October we took our ribbons off, but we didn't throw them away.

"This campaign is going to have to go on and on," said Mom.

Mom had a few weeks' rest after she'd finished her chemotherapy. Then she started six weeks of radiation treatment. The dreariest thing was that she had to go to the hospital every day from Mondays to Fridays. They gave her the weekends off. The doctor drew marks on her chest with a felt-tip pen, to show exactly where the radiation treatment was going to be aimed. She had to be careful not to wash them off, and if they got faint she had to draw them on again. Sometimes she'd open the bathroom door and shout down the stairs for Dad to come and redraw the marks where she couldn't reach.

Dad used to chuckle about it. "I've been asked to do some strange things in my time," he said, "but this must be the strangest!"

Mom said at first that the radiation was much easier than the chemotherapy.

"Does it hurt?" I asked my usual question.

Mom shook her head.

"Well, what happens then?"

"You have to lie down on a rather hard sort of bed and once they've got you in the right position, the radiographers scuttle out of the room and switch the machine on. Just like an ordinary X ray. The machine goes beep, beep, beep, and they rush back in and help you get up."

"Doesn't sound too bad," I said.

But as the weeks went by she began to feel tired, and her skin got sore as though she'd been in the sun too long.

"The thing with sunburn is that you can keep out of the sun once you've got it," she complained. "I've got to keep on going to the hospital for more. Still, I know that everyone else is finding it hard, too. There was a woman crying in the waiting room today."

"Oh, how awful," I said.

Mom sighed and smiled. "There's often somebody crying," she said. "But we help one another. We get out tissues and hold hands, and tell them that we all feel the same."

*   *   *

I came down one Sunday morning and found Mom in the kitchen surrounded by piles of washing, some clean, some dirty. The sink was stacked high with dishes that needed doing, and Mom stood there in the middle of it all with tears pouring down her cheeks.

"What's wrong?" I said. It didn't look much different to me. Every Sunday was like that.

"What's wrong?" she yelled, going quite red in the face. "What's wrong? The whole house is filthy! There's mountains of washing and ironing! There's meals to cook and pots to wash! And I feel terrible!"

She sobbed and I just stared at her, wondering what on earth to do.

"Look at it all!" she cried, snatching up dirty clothes and towels and throwing them around.

"What's up?" said Dad, coming along behind me. "What's all the noise about?"

Johnny came in through the back door. "What's wrong with Mommy?" he asked, looking scared.

"Everything!" shrieked Mom. "The whole place is a mess! And I can't sort it out."

"It's all right . . . it's all right," said Dad, going up to her and putting his arms around her. "We'll deal with it. You go and sit down in the front room. We'll get all the jobs done."

Mom cried all the more then, but she allowed us to lead her into the front room.

"I'm just fed up with it all," she sobbed. "When you're ill at first everyone makes a fuss. Look at all the flowers and cards I got. Now everyone's bored with me being ill—but I feel worse than ever."

I did begin to see what she meant.

I ran up to my bedroom and brought down all my fashion magazines for Mom to read. Dad went to make her a cup of tea, and Johnny disappeared into the garden. He came back with a bunch of rather brown late roses and straggly snapdragons.

"Brought you some flowers," he said.

That made Mom's tears flow all over again, but she was smiling as well.

"That's better," she said, calming down and hugging Johnny. "I'm feeling better now. These are the best flowers I've ever had. Sorry to be so ratty, but it's just such hard work. It's damned hard work getting through all this."

Then we left her to read the magazines and sip her tea while we set to work and sorted out the house.

We had the washing machine going all day, and we scrubbed and polished and wiped and washed until everything was clean and smelling nice.

"I'm worn out and starving," I told Dad.

"So'm I," he agreed.

"Who's going to cook?" I asked.

We looked at each other for a moment, then burst out laughing.

"Chinese takeout," said Dad.

"Oh, yes. Sweet and sour shrimp, curry, and rice."

* * *

It was Christmas by the time Mom had finished all her treatments. Gradually through January and February our life seemed to slowly return to normal. Mom had to keep going to the hospital for checkups, but she was soon busy working at the shop full-time with Dad.

Once a month she started going to the breast cancer support group meetings.

I made a face. "Sounds really depressing. A whole gang of women who've all had breast cancer?"

"It's the opposite of depressing," she said.

"But what do you do?"

"Well, we talk and try to help one another. Boy, do we talk! But most of them are incredibly busy, raising money for cancer research and funds for a telephone hotline. Two of the women are rappelling down the side of the hospital next week. Do you want to sponsor them?"

My mouth dropped open. "What? From the top?" Mom laughed and nodded.

"Can we watch?" I asked.

Soon after Easter, we started making plans for our summer vacation once again.

EPILOGUE

It was the last afternoon of school, just before the holidays. We cheered at lunchtime because lessons had ended. I went off with Laura into the girls' changing room, and we struggled into our vase dance costumes, slightly altered to accommodate a year's growth. Then we wandered out to Ellspring Wood.

Two beautiful pictures stood at the back of the well, set into panels of damp worked clay. The art department had been busy with them for weeks.

One picture showed a tall woman dressed in a gown made from purple cranesbill petals and red campions. On her head was a golden crown worked with delicate petals from buttercups. She was St. Helen, Yorkshire-born empress, mother of the great emperor Constantine. Next to her was another panel that Corrie had insisted upon. A woman, dressed in a gown of tiny creamy elderflowers and fresh green leaves, her head crowned with a simple wreath of delicate pink bog rosemary. She carried a strong staff, symbol of the wayfarer. Ellen of the Ways looked quiet and mysterious beside the strong royal colors of St. Helen, but I thought she was very beautiful. The art department had done us proud.

Then slowly a crowd gathered. The school orchestra

brought out their instruments and set themselves up on the sloping hillside. The school choir trooped out to join us and parents and grandparents with lots of little kids flocked in. The photographer from the *Evening News* came again, and this time he took photographs of us as we performed our vase dance. The school orchestra played Debussy's lovely, trickly music. Then Mrs. Jones made a speech about the well and how thankful we should be for fresh, clean water, even in these days of taps and water companies. Then the choir sang and everyone clapped and cheered.

Mom and Dad were there with Johnny, clapping with the rest. Mom came rushing up to hug me. "You were wonderful," she said. "I'm so glad I saw your dance at last."

Dad wanted to drive through the night to avoid heavy traffic, so that evening we all crammed into our car, including Laura. Mom drove the first half of the journey and we slept most of the way, then Dad took over. We woke up feeling a little tired and grumpy. But we didn't stay grumpy long, for as dawn came, we saw that we were traveling along beside a beautiful stretch of blue sea and golden sand. The jumbled rooftops of St. Ives glimmered in the morning sunlight.

Mom turned to Dad and kissed him on the cheek.

"What was that for?" he asked, smiling.

"Because it's going to be the best vacation ever," she said.

Later that afternoon, when we'd gotten through the chaos of taking over our apartment and unpacking our things, we wandered onto the little beach. Johnny stripped down to his shorts and ran off into the sea.

"Oh, heavens!" said Mom. "Will he be all right?"

Dad yawned and shook his head. "I'm too tired to go chasing after him."

"I'll keep my eye on him," Laura said, getting up obligingly.

As she wandered off, I wondered if I should go with her, but I just wanted to sit there for a moment with Mom and Dad. There we were at last, on the little beach that had somehow helped Mom to get through all that dreary chemotherapy.

She sighed and echoed my thoughts. "When I imagined myself here," she said, "it wasn't crowded or littered or chilly, but it's so good to be sitting on the real beach at last."

I nodded. "The real thing's more exciting and more smelly, too!"

Mom laughed, but then she put her arm around my shoulders. "It's been so difficult getting through this year," she said. "It's been hard for you, too, I can see that. But somehow this feels like a fresh start—a new beginning. I know now what the most precious thing on earth is."

"What?" I asked.

"I think it's just . . . being alive," she said. "We mustn't waste a minute of it."

I leaned my cheek against hers.

"No . . . we won't," I said.